How many medical positions could there be in a community this size?

Though Ben didn't want to ask, he had to. "What position, if you don't mind my asking?"

"Clinical Director of the Community Outreach Clinic. It's a new program," Sara explained. "They're trying to reach the outlying, underserved rural population and seasonal workers and their families." Excitement lit her eyes as she spoke.

Ben nodded. Oh, he was well versed in the vision for the new clinic, all right. Sara's enthusiasm was well-placed. The entire project stirred a professional anticipation and energy he hadn't felt in a very long time.

"I've been waiting years for this clinic to become a reality," she said.

The earnestness in her voice brought his own doubts tumbling out. Hadn't the Lord led him to Paradise and this job?

Ben met her gaze head-on. "Um, Sara. There's something you ought to know."

She cocked her head in question. "What's that?"

"I'm in Paradise interviewing for the same position."

Books by Tina Radcliffe

Love Inspired

The Rancher's Reunion
Oklahoma Reunion
Mending the Doctor's Heart

TINA RADCLIFFE

has been dreaming and scribbling for years. Originally from Western New York, she left home for a tour of duty with the Army Security Agency stationed in Augsburg, Germany, and ended up in Tulsa, Oklahoma. While living in Tulsa she spent ten years as a certified oncology R.N. A former library cataloger, she now works for a large mail-order pharmacy. Tina currently resides in the foothills of Colorado, where she writes heartwarming romance. You can reach her at www.tinaradcliffe.com.

Mending the Doctor's Heart

Tina Radcliffe

Recycling programs for this product may not exist in your area.

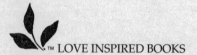

™ LOVE INSPIRED BOOKS

ISBN-13: 978-0-373-81687-3

MENDING THE DOCTOR'S HEART

Copyright © 2013 by Tina M. Radcliffe

www.LoveInspiredBooks.com

Printed in U.S.A.

Once upon a time I was blessed to work as an Oncology Certified R.N. in Tulsa, Oklahoma, at Camelot, also known as the City of Faith Hospital. This book is dedicated to all the wonderful, Christian nurses, doctors, aides, techs and support staff who saved lives and shared the Gospel during their shifts.

To Sharon Medley, thank you for reading my first chapters and giving me your honest feedback. As always, thank you to my husband, Tom, who never tires of the signs on my office door telling him 'Do Not Disturb, Writing In Progress.' Of course it takes a village; in my case that village is called Seekerville: Mary, Ruthy, Debby, Julie, Sandra, Missy, Audra, Janet, Cara, Myra, Pam and Glynna. Thank you, sisters in the Lord, for your support.

Many thanks to my editor, Rachel Burkot, who blesses me with her discerning editorial eye and her cheerful heart, and who makes me a better writer. A final thank-you to my supportive agent Meredith Bernstein, who always makes me feel like a champion.

Chapter One

Welcome to Paradise.

Ben Rogers stared at the glossy white sign posted in front of a row of tall Colorado conifers.

Paradise? Doubtful.

Salvation? Possibly.

He shook his head and chuckled.

At least he still had a sense of humor. That was pretty much all he'd taken with him from Denver, besides his leather medical bag and whatever fit in his Land Rover. His future lay beyond the welcome sign that boasted a population of seventeen hundred.

Ben guided his vehicle around an enormous pothole and straight into the heart of the small mountain town. Paradise, Colorado, was nestled in the San Luis Valley, with the Sangre De Cristo Mountains to the north and the San Juan Mountains to the west. At eight thousand feet, the elevation of Paradise was even higher than Denver's fifty-two eighty.

The mountains provided a picturesque backdrop for the shops that lined the main thoroughfare and the sidewalks dotted with wrought-iron benches and masses of bright summer flowers that overflowed sidewalk pots.

Carolyn would have loved Paradise.

Ben winced, then rubbed a hand across his face. Six months had passed since he'd lost her, but he continued to see the world through his little sister's eyes.

His stomach growled, offering a distraction. After a four-hour drive he was starving. A glance at the clock on the dash confirmed there was just enough time to grab something to eat before he retrieved the key to his rental cabin and headed to an appointment with his new boss, the medical director of the Paradise Community Hospital. He pulled into an open parking spot along the curb and glanced around.

Would it be The Prospector restaurant, or Patti Jo's Café and Bakery? Ben stepped out of the Land Rover and inhaled.

Cinnamon rolls?

The tantalizing aromas of butter, cinnamon and vanilla lured him to a quaint shop with etched-glass windows.

Oh, yeah. Patti Jo's won, hands down.

Tinkling bells sounded as he opened the bright crimson door. Before him, customers patiently stood in line at the single cash register, most perusing the glass cases filled with pastries as they waited. Ben scanned the small room, noting that every single bistro table and red leather booth was occupied.

Waiting wasn't his strong suit. Maybe he'd try the restaurant instead.

He turned to leave just as an elderly man seated at a table to his far left began to cough. Mere moments later, the man stood and clutched his throat before he stumbled back from the table. The coughing stopped, and his face took on a blue tinge.

Without thinking, adrenaline surging, Ben pushed forward through the customers.

But not soon enough.

The man crumpled, striking his head on the table edge as he spiraled down to the floor. Ben reached him and automatically slid his fingers along the victim's neck.

Pulse still strong. *Thank You, God.*

He placed his ear to the man's chest.

Air movement negligent.

Tilting the man's head, Ben searched his mouth for an obstruction. None evident. Yet something had occluded his airway.

"Everyone step back." Ben turned to a waitress and nodded toward the silver-haired woman who hovered close. "Can you help her to a chair?"

He made purposeful eye contact with the cashier, a young girl whose face was pale, her eyes rounded.

"What's your name?" Ben asked, while quickly positioning himself behind the barely conscious man.

"Susan."

The girl's frantic glances darted back and forth from the man on the floor and then to him again.

"Susan, look at me," he commanded. "I need you to call 9-1-1. *Right now.* Okay?"

She nodded and pulled a cell phone from her smock pocket.

Arms around the fallen man's waist, Ben gave a practiced abdominal thrust. Once. Twice. Three times. The air pressure action caused something to dislodge and shoot from the man's mouth into the air. A sharp sucking inhalation filled the now-silent room before the man coughed, and then began normal respirations.

"That's it," he encouraged. "Just breathe. I've got you."

A collective sound of relief fluttered through the small crowd.

Ben's own breathing slowed now that the crisis was over. For a moment he simply rested on his haunches, stunned with the realization that he'd just responded to an emergency like his old self. There'd been zero time for second thoughts, self-doubting or the crippling panic attacks.

He swallowed hard and took a deep breath. *Thank You, Lord. Thank You.*

Easing the elderly man away from him, Ben began a quick inspection of his head, parting the gray hairs where blood oozed from a scalp wound.

"I've got gauze for that laceration."

Ben turned, his gaze slamming into the clear green eyes of a petite dark-haired woman, about his age. She reached a latex-gloved hand forward and applied pressure to the victim's head.

"Thanks," Ben murmured, grateful for the assist.

After a minute, the woman lifted the corner of the now blood-saturated gauze.

He peered at the site. "Not too bad."

"Nothing a couple sutures won't fix," she said.

Surprised, Ben glanced over his shoulder and gave a nod of agreement at her words. Her confident demeanor said she obviously had a medical background.

Before he could consider that further, the siren of an emergency vehicle echoed. The sound became louder and louder until two paramedics burst through the door of the shop.

As they strode toward him, Ben carefully

rose to transfer the care of the victim for a complete evaluation.

"Choking incident. Resolved with Heimlich." Ben addressed the uniformed medics. "Minor scalp laceration, approximately one-eighth centimeter, secondary to head trauma."

He turned away, relieved that everyone's attention was on the victim, which allowed him to slip to the front door.

As he turned away, the elderly woman who'd been with the fallen man grabbed Ben's arm.

"Thank you, son," she said. "You saved my husband's life." Her soft eyes overflowed with emotion as they met his.

"You're welcome, ma'am."

Head bowed, Ben collected himself. He'd doubted himself for so long; the simple thank you touched a place inside that desperately needed affirmation. Maybe God *could* still use him.

When he looked up, his eyes met the familiar gaze of the woman who'd assisted him. She pulled hand sanitizer from a first-aid kit that now sat on the café table and squeezed some liquid into her palm before handing the bottle to him.

"Here you go, Doc."

"Thanks. How'd you know I'm a doctor?"

"Would you believe it takes one to know one?" Amusement skittered across her face.

"Really?" Ben smiled. As he cleaned his hands, he noted with interest her red-plaid Western shirt, well-worn and snug jeans and scuffed cowboy boots. A doctor, huh?

"I'm Sara Elliott. Dr. Sara Elliott."

"Ben Rogers. Nice to meet you."

He couldn't resist a further assessment, from the sprinkling of light freckles that dusted her small nose to the teasing smile that touched her lips and reached her eyes. There was something about the pint-sized beauty that sharpened his senses.

"Nice job with Orvis."

"Orvis?"

"Orvis Carter. His daughter-in-law owns this café."

Ben nodded as he digested the information. When his gaze met Sara's and held for a long moment, he was surprised at the connection between them. *Or had he imagined it?*

Flustered, Sara Elliott pushed a thick, dark braid over her shoulder and shoved a few loose tendrils of hair back from her face. No, she seemed as taken off guard as he was.

The slight tilting of her head revealed a long, thin scar running from her temple to her ear, parallel with her hairline. It was obvious from the silvery shade and flattened texture that it was years old.

Curious.

Ben looked away, then slid his phone from his pocket, grimacing when he saw the time. "I hate to Heimlich and run, but I've got to be somewhere."

He pushed open the door of the shop and moved the conversation past the still-lingering crowd and the paramedics who were finishing up, out to the sidewalk.

"No problem." She followed him outside. "I'm sure we'll meet again. Paradise is a small town."

"Do you live here?"

"I grew up in Paradise." She tucked a strand of hair behind her ear and leaned closer, her voice conspiratorial. "But the truth is, I'm here about a job."

"Oh?" Ben froze, his mind calculating. How many medical positions could there be in a community this size? He'd done his homework. Paradise Hospital itself only had four physicians on staff, and there were a handful of family-practice physicians scattered throughout the valley.

Though he didn't want to ask, he had to. "What position, if you don't mind my asking?"

"Clinical Director of the Community Outreach Clinic."

This time his brows shot up. If Sara took the response as confusion, she was right.

Almost.

"It's a new program," she explained. "They're trying to reach the outlying, underserved rural population and seasonal workers and their families." Excitement lit her eyes as she spoke. "There's also a plan for a clinic team to assist during severe weather emergencies that can hit the valley and the foothills."

Ben nodded. Oh, he was well versed in the goals, the budget and the vision for the new clinic, all right. Yeah, Sara's enthusiasm was well placed. The entire project stirred a professional anticipation and energy he hadn't felt in a very long time.

"I've been waiting years for this clinic to become a reality," she said.

The earnestness in her voice brought his own doubts tumbling out. Hadn't the Lord led him to Paradise and this job?

Ben met her gaze head-on. "Um, Sara. There's something you ought to know."

She cocked her head in question. "What's that?"

"I'm in Paradise interviewing for the same position."

Sara opened her mouth then closed it. *Not really?*

She looked at Ben. His chocolate-brown eyes were unwavering, and the expression on his face said he was very serious.

That didn't make sense. The director position had been all but given to her.

She glanced at the tall, lean man in front of her again, scrutinizing his reserved expression, doing her best to ignore his appeal in the expensive black polo shirt and crisp tan chinos.

"Awkward," Ben murmured. He ran a hand

through his well-kept dark hair and shook his head.

"I'll say." His discomfort only matched her own. "So, you're meeting with the medical director today?" she asked.

"A Dr. Rhoades? Yeah." Once again he glanced at his phone. "I've really got to get going. Been on the road for hours. I need a quick shower and change of clothes."

"Where are you staying?"

"I've rented a place."

Sara blinked. "Already?"

He shrugged. "Obviously there was some miscommunication."

"You've quit your job, as well?"

"No, I've been on a…sabbatical."

Was that a flash of pain she saw in his eyes before he looked away? There was obviously a story to be told. One he wasn't going to share with a stranger.

"And you?" he asked. "You said you grew up here."

"I did, but I live in Boulder. I've been back for several weeks now. My father had a cardiac incident."

Ben furrowed his brows. "I'm sorry to hear that. He's okay?"

"What he is is stubborn." Sara shook her head. "My reason for moving back to Paradise."

He took a step toward the curb. "That's admirable."

"Hardly, but let's not even go there." Sara waved a hand in the air. "Besides, you have to get going."

His eyes widened a fraction, but she ignored the question on his face.

"What time is your appointment?" she asked.

"Two." He pulled car keys from his pocket.

"I'm meeting with him at three."

"I see. Well, ah, good luck, then."

"Thanks. You, too."

Ben seemed to hesitate, glancing down at the sidewalk, then up before he spoke again. "Sara."

The pleasant sound of her name on his lips surprised her. "Yes?" she asked as their gazes connected.

"No matter how it turns out, it was nice to have met you."

She paused at the words, her response a breathless, "Thank you."

With a crooked smile, he turned away.

Sara followed his easy gait as he walked down the street.

Oh, no, no. This was not good.

She shook her head. They'd just met, and not only had Ben Rogers disturbed her plans for the future, but he was disturbing her peace of mind, as well.

She pulled her cell from her back pocket and punched speed dial. "Is Dr. Rhoades available? This is Sara Elliott calling."

A long minute later she heard a familiar voice.

"Sara, what can I do for you?"

"Uncle Henry, what's going on?" She tucked the phone beneath her ear and shoulder while she unlocked her ancient Jeep and yanked open the recalcitrant door on the driver's side.

"You'll have to be more specific, my dear."

She slid into the vehicle. "I just met Ben Rogers. Dr. Ben Rogers."

Henry Rhoades's voice perked up. "Ah, yes, and what did you think?"

"Think? We'll he's a little stuffy, but I'm willing to overlook that since he just saved Orvis Carter's life at Patti Jo's."

"Orvis? At the café, you say? Most commendable."

"Yes. It certainly is." Sara put the key into the ignition and hit the window button, allowing the summer breeze to cool her skin. "The thing is, Uncle Henry, Ben Rogers says he's here about the clinic director job."

The line was quiet before her uncle cleared his throat. "Yes, well, I'll sort it all out."

"Sort it out? Uncle Henry, you never even told me there was another candidate." She released a frustrated breath. "Be straight with me. Is my father involved in this?"

"Your father has made a substantial donation to the clinic building project, if that's what you mean."

"I mean, did my father make you offer me the position?" She paused, confused. "And how did my father get involved in funding the clinic?"

"You know, Sara, the entire situation is rather complicated."

She groaned and leaned back against the headrest. "Oh, Uncle Henry."

"Now, Sara, you're getting all worked up for nothing. The fact is, the clinic was in dire need of funds for the final phase, and I went to your father for assistance."

"And he said yes? But that doesn't make sense. He's always been adamantly against me becoming a physician, always blaming Mom's medical career for the accident. Why would he agree to have anything to do with the clinic project?"

"He didn't. At first."

Sara released a soft gasp. "Until his heart attack."

Again the silence stretched before her uncle finally spoke.

"Try to understand, Sara. The last two years since you've been gone have been very difficult for your father. He's paid penance for his sins. I believe he's willing to do anything to keep his daughter in Paradise."

"What you mean is, he tried to buy me a husband and that didn't work, so now he's buying me a career."

"Don't jump to conclusions. Things are not exactly what you think."

She slapped the steering wheel with an open palm. The truth was, things *were* exactly as she thought. Sara bit her lip. There was no point taking out her frustration on her uncle. Hollis Elliott had struck again. No doubt her uncle was between a rock and a hard place.

"I should withdraw my application."

"Don't be ridiculous. You'll be evaluated on your merit, you know that. If I had realized you were seriously contemplating a permanent move back to Paradise, I would have told you about the position straight away, instead of waiting for Hollis to make the suggestion. But considering your departure…"

"I know. I know." Sara closed her eyes. "You don't have to say it. I let you down last time, and I'm sorry."

Henry Rhoades continued, "I have Dr. Rogers scheduled for 2 p.m. Why don't you come by shortly after that?"

"What are you up to?"

"Why, nothing. No worries, dear."

No worries? Well, she was worried. Very worried, because the last time her father had interfered in her life she'd lost everything, and she wasn't ready for that to happen again.

The Lord had led her back to Paradise; she could only pray He would give her the courage to stay this time.

Chapter Two

Ben cranked up the air-conditioning in the Land Rover to subzero and leaned back against the leather seat as he stared at the cluster of buildings that made up the medical quadrant. He wiped his palms on his dark slacks and took a deep breath. Dr. Rhoades's office was in the administrative building adjacent to the hospital. Not actually in the hospital at all.

I can do this.

Sure he could. Because otherwise, how was he going to explain that he was a highly credentialed internist with hospital phobia?

Ben adjusted his tie and slid out of the vehicle. He was a professional, and this wasn't rational. Yeah, he knew that in his heart as well as his head, but the anxiety attacks didn't pay much attention to rationale.

Focused, he walked up the covered walkway, into the lobby and the elevator and pushed the button.

Elevators. Why couldn't he get sweaty palms and heart palpitations when he entered closed spaces? Claustrophobia was acceptable. Nosocomephobia, the fear of hospitals? Not so much.

A blonde receptionist in a floating ivory dress smiled and took his name.

"Dr. Rhoades will see you shortly. Make yourself at home. Oh, and Dr. Rogers, welcome to Paradise."

"Ah, thank you." So why did he suddenly feel like he was waiting for admission to the Pearly Gates?

The urge to bolt welled up inside of him. Tamping down anxiety, Ben rubbed the back of his neck as he paced back and forth, inspecting the framed photos of the hospital staff on the white walls.

He knew when he applied for the position that this day would come. But was he ready?

Actually getting the job seemed as terrifying as the possibility of being turned down.

"Dr. Rogers, you may go in now."

Ben swallowed hard and adjusted his tie one last time before crossing the threshold to Medical Director Dr. Henry Rhoades's sanctum. Floor-to-ceiling windows stretched along the far side of the room, ushering in streams of sunlight and offering an unobstructed view of the mountain peaks in the distance. Distracted by the scenery, Ben was taken by surprise when a robust silver-haired gentleman in a wheelchair stopped in front of him.

Dr. Rhoades?

The man in the chair wore a crisp blue shirt with the sleeves haphazardly shoved up to reveal muscular forearms. His striped navy tie was slightly askew.

"Dr. Rogers." He struck out a hand. "Delighted to finally meet you."

Henry Rhoades's grin lit up his round face. The man's smile and the bright green eyes behind his wire-rimmed spectacles seemed somewhat familiar, but Ben couldn't quite place why.

"Thank you, sir," he said.

"I heard about your heroics at the café. Well done."

"Hardly heroics, sir. Dislodged a chocolate-chunk cookie. The Friday special, I understand."

Dr. Rhoades chuckled. "None the less, it only reaffirms your curriculum vitae. Exemplary."

"Thank you."

"You met Dr. Elliott, as well."

Ben frowned, confused. How could the man possibly know he'd met Sara Elliott less than two hours ago?

Henry Rhoades wheeled himself behind the large oak desk with practiced ease and picked up a file. "Please have a seat. Relax."

Following instructions, Ben did his best imitation of relaxing. "Yes, we did meet, and I have to admit that after talking to her, I'm a little confused. My last conversation with you indicated the final interview was, well…"

"A formality."

"Yes, sir."

"At the time I spoke to you, that's exactly

what it was, and as I said, your credentials are excellent. You were my first choice."

Were?

"But I'll get to that in a moment." Dr. Rhoades glanced down at the now open folder on his desk. "Tell me about this sabbatical you've been on."

Ben took a calming breath. "My sister died six months ago. I needed a break."

"Your sister." Henry Rhoades paused, taken aback for a moment. "My condolences."

When the older man narrowed his eyes and stared at him, Ben realized he was seeing far too much. He glanced away from the perceptive gaze and instead watched the play of dappled light that streamed in through the window, its prism bending as it reached out and landed on a silver picture frame on the desk. The picture was of a young child and a woman laughing.

Dr. Rhoades cleared his throat and continued. "Loss is never easy. Are you sure you're ready to get back to work?"

"Sir, I'm committed to giving you one hundred percent."

"Fair enough."

For a moment, the only sound was the rhythmic ticking of a large antique clock on a bookshelf.

"Well now, let's get to the point. Dr. Elliott's father has become the benefactor for the new clinic. The project seemed stalled in perpetuity—until he stepped in."

Sara Elliott's father? Ben tried to wrap his mind around that bomb of information.

"I see." What did he see? That his chance at redemption was being cancelled out by a bankroll? The gates to Paradise were closing fast, and he'd barely gotten his foot inside. *He had to do something.*

"The timing of this has me puzzled," Ben admitted.

"Understandable. I apologize for that." Dr. Rhoades removed his glasses, wiped a spot from the lens with his tie, and then slid them back on the bridge of his nose. "Hollis Elliott suffered a cardiac arrest less than a month ago. When Sara returned home, naturally her father saw a window of opportunity for his only child to remain in Paradise. Unfortunately it was only a few days ago that he notified me of his wishes, and by then the candidates for the position had already been narrowed down to you."

Ben took a deep breath. So where did that leave him in the equation? One plus one was still two as far as he could tell, and there was only a single open position.

Henry Rhoades frowned for moment. "I trust you will keep what I'm about to say confidential."

"Yes, sir."

"I've been the medical director here in Paradise for over twenty-five years. One thing I have learned is that sometimes it's better to proceed and apologize later than ask permission." He winked, and once again Ben couldn't shake the feeling that he'd seen that mischievous glimmer before.

"Sir?"

"Stay with me for a moment. I do eventually arrive at my destination."

Ben nodded, amused and concerned at the same time. This was like no other job interview he could remember. Physician interviews were generally so starched, he could barely breathe. Yet Dr. Henry Rhoades was about as laid-back as they come, leaving Ben struggling to figure the man out, much less where the convoluted conversation would lead.

"Bequeaths and donations go directly to the hospital foundation, which is overseen by the Board of Trustees. The clinic is under that same board, so I have gone to them for assistance in resolving this situation. While Hollis Elliott's generous funding has made the last phase of the clinic project possible, I am not without options."

The phone on his desk buzzed.

"Excuse me." He picked up the receiver. "Yes. Thank you. Send her in."

The door opened, and Sara Elliott walked into the room.

Sara had changed clothes and now wore a simple yet elegant navy dress, her long hair free and flowing. This was quite a transformation from the cowgirl he'd met earlier.

Surprised, Ben caught his breath before he immediately stood. And stumbled.

Way to go, Rogers. Grace under pressure.

"Are you all right?" she murmured.

"Yeah. The carpet tripped me." He adjusted his suit coat and cleared his throat.

A soft laugh tumbled from her lips. "Happens to me all the time."

"Sara, my dear." Henry Rhoades smiled. "You've met Dr. Rogers."

"I have."

Ben paused and cocked his head at the warm tone in Dr. Rhoades's conversation with Sara. A warning bell sounded somewhere, but he dismissed it. After all, Paradise was a small town, and her father *was,* after all, the financier behind the clinic.

"I had the opportunity to see Dr. Rogers in action today," she continued.

"Yes, and no doubt he will be on the front page of the *Paradise Observer,*" Dr. Rhoades said with a nod toward him.

Sara smiled as her gaze met Ben's. "Don't let it go to your head."

Ben blinked. Surely they weren't serious.

Once Sara had settled in the leather Windsor wing chair next to his, Ben sat down again.

Henry Rhoades steepled his fingers and assessed them both over the rim of his glasses. "Now then, the matter at hand is the clinic position. What I'm proposing is that you work together this summer."

Sara's eyes widened as she looked from Dr. Rhoades to him. "Together?" She slowly repeated the word that had lodged in Ben's own throat.

From directing a clinic to job sharing in less than thirty minutes.

"Yes," Dr. Rhoades answered. "I've spoken to the board, and they are willing to subsidize two doctors through the first of September. At that time we'll assess our options."

"That's a little over eight weeks from now. Are you saying we're going to *share* the position for the entire eight weeks?" Sara asked, her tone incredulous.

"Since the clinic officially opens late September, there's more than enough work to keep you both busy. Interviewing medical staff. Ordering supplies. Then there's accreditation. I can assure you the time will pass very quickly."

"I don't know," she murmured. "A lot can happen in eight weeks."

"Precisely," Dr. Rhoades responded with an enthusiastic wag of his index finger. "Think of this as a personal and professional due diligence. Paradise needs someone who's ready to commit to a future here."

Pink now tinged Sara's high cheekbones. She grimaced and clasped her hands tightly in her lap.

"Eight weeks is plenty of opportunity to discover whether Paradise is a good fit for you and if you're a good fit for Paradise, wouldn't you say, Dr. Rogers?"

Confused at the subtle undercurrent, Ben slowly looked from Sara to Henry Rhoades before clearing his throat and agreeing. "Yes, sir."

What else could he say? Paradise was slipping through his fingers, and he couldn't… no, he flat-out refused to allow that to happen.

"Excellent." Dr. Rhoades closed the folder on his desk. "You're scheduled for Human Resources processing Monday, and then I'll see you at the clinic on Tuesday. Dress casually. While the construction is basically complete, there is still quite a bit of dust and dirt."

Ben nodded, but his head continued to spin as he stood. What had just happened? This wasn't the outcome he'd hoped for, packed up his belongings and driven hours for.

"Have you eaten?" the older man asked.

"Sir?"

"Have you eaten?"

"Almost," Ben responded.

"Almost?" Dr. Rhoades raised a bushy brow.

"I was headed to Patti Jo's and never quite made it to a table."

"Sara, take Dr. Rogers to The Prospector."

Sara nodded, but didn't appear any more enthused than he felt at the moment.

"I don't want to impose," Ben interjected.

"Nonsense. I'd take you myself, but I've got a previous commitment. Besides, you two should get to know each other since you'll be working very closely together for eight weeks."

Eight weeks.

Was that enough time to convince Henry Rhoades that he was the right person for the job?

Ben wanted the position more than ever. His troubled spirit had been soothed the moment he drove into the small town. Now he just had to make sure he got what he wanted.

Sara bit her lip and glanced quickly at Ben once they were seated. "I'm really sorry about this. I never expected that we'd be…" She paused, at a loss for words.

Ben shrugged. "Not exactly what I expected either, but hardly your fault."

She fiddled with her napkin, grateful when their waitress approached them and slid a stoneware bowl of homemade pickles on the polished pine table.

"What do you recommend?" Ben asked, turning over the menu.

"The valley is known for their beef and bison." Sara placed an order for a bison burger and handed her menu to the server.

"I'll have the same thing," he said.

She looked around at the rustic décor as if seeing it for the first time before meeting Ben's eyes.

He gave a tight-lipped smile but said nothing.

"So you went to school in Colorado?" Sara asked, eager to ease the palpable tension between them.

"University of Colorado," Ben said. "You?"

"Baylor."

"Baylor?" He gave a thoughtful, self-satisfied nod, the implication clear.

Money. That was laughable.

Did he think she was a trust-fund baby? If only. No, she'd financed her education all by herself. At this point, the huge debt from medical school and residency was a tidy sum, the balance of which could probably cover the purchase of a small island in the Caribbean.

"Baylor is sort of a family tradition," she murmured.

When Ben gave her yet another stiff nod, she put a smile on her face, determined to be polite, at least until the meal was over. She bit into a crisp, sweet pickle and concentrated on the burst of flavor instead of the man in front of her.

"Your father is a physician?" he asked.

"My father is a rancher," Sara said.

"Ah, local beef." He pinned her with his gaze. "How'd you end up in medicine?"

She slowly wiped her lips with her napkin. "My mother was a pediatrician."

"Was?"

"I lost her when I was very young."

Ben's eyes clouded with concern, and he glanced away. "I'm…I'm very sorry." The subtle antagonism in his voice vanished.

"Thank you." Sara paused. "What about your parents?"

"My father is a general practitioner, and my mother is a nurse. They've been big on rural medicine all my life. Every vacation from school was a mini-mission trip."

"You were fortunate."

"Probably, but I didn't think so at the time," Ben said.

"I've spent most of my life in Paradise and the rest wishing I was back here." She gave a small laugh. "I guess you just don't appreciate some things until they're gone."

Her words hung between them for a moment before Ben answered.

"I guess you're right."

She took a long sip of her water and set her glass down. Ben's direct gaze met hers.

"May I ask about Dr. Rhoades's medical condition?"

"Incomplete paraplegia." Her finger traced the moisture on the glass over and over as she spoke. "It was a car accident, many years ago. Emergency medical response couldn't get to the vehicle due to a snowstorm."

Ben inhaled sharply.

"Another reason why the outreach clinic is so important to him."

Ben nodded slowly.

Her cell rang, and she dug in her purse. "It's my father. Do you mind if I take it?"

"No. Of course not."

"Dad, everything okay?" Sara looked toward Ben and then away. "Yes, I've met with Uncle Henry. I'll be home soon. We can talk then. I have to go now."

Shaking her head, she put the phone away.

"Dr. Rhoades is your uncle." Ben's voice was flat and tight, the words punctuated with a nameless accusation.

Their meals were set in front of them, and Sara waited until the waitress left before responding.

"He is my uncle. But it's not what you think—"

"It's not?" His brows shot up. "How do you figure?"

"Ben, Dr. Rhoades is going to hire the right person for the job."

He stared through her, his jaw rigid. "You mean Uncle Henry?"

"There's no need to be condescending, Dr. Rogers."

Ben released a frustrated breath. "Look, maybe you think I'm being harsh, but consider the situation from where I'm sitting. Your father subsidized the project, and your uncle manages the program. Those are the facts, correct?"

She nodded.

"What I don't understand is why your uncle doesn't just hire you. Why not let me down now instead of eight weeks from now?"

The thick burger and hot fries in front of her suddenly lost their appeal. Sara sighed and pushed aside the large white platter. "Because last time he hired me, I left him high and dry."

The long silence between them stretched, until Ben finally spoke.

"You quit?"

"It's not something I'm proud of, but yes. I was on staff at the hospital, and I broke my contract and resigned."

"When was this?"

"Two years ago."

"I guess I *don't* understand."

"All you need to know is that I'm not the front-runner for this position. You may think I have the home-team advantage, but clearly you are my uncle's first choice."

He raised his palms. "So what's changed in twenty-four months?"

Sara swallowed the bitterness rising in her throat. "My father's heart attack made me realize that as much as he exasperates me, I'm still his daughter. His only child. And I love him. So I've got to try to put the past—my mistakes and his—behind me and move on." She folded her hands tightly in her lap. "That also means I need to find a way to make peace with him."

Ben stared at her for moments, his lips a grim line. "Sometimes the answer is to simply give the situation to God. Turn it over to Him and trust that He can find a way."

Sara was silent, surprised by his faithful words and by the way his gaze searched hers. She glanced away.

"That's a huge step of faith," she murmured before looking up again. "Do you really think that the Lord can find a way when things are such a mess?"

"I'm banking on it," Ben said. He inhaled and then slowly exhaled. "So I guess we've both got a lot invested in the next eight weeks."

An awkward tension once again settled between them.

Ben looked from her untouched dinner to his own. "Maybe we could call a time-out," he finally said. "Because I'm really starving."

She shook her head at the plea in his voice, then inched her plate close again, picking up her napkin and silverware. "This doesn't have to be adversarial, you know."

"Perhaps not, but make no mistake. I want that position, Sara."

She peeked at him from beneath her lashes.

Yes, he wanted the position, but there was more going on here. Why was the position so important to him? And what exactly was Ben Rogers running from?

He had more than his own share of secrets. She recognized a wounded soul in the tall, lean physician. Whether he knew it or not, she suspected he was on his own mission trip right now.

Eight weeks. Was it enough time to find

out what was going on behind those sad eyes? She sure could use an ally if she was going to find the courage to stay. Ben might just be that ally.

Could it be they needed each other as much as they needed Paradise? That possibility worried her more than anything, especially since every time her gaze met his, she glimpsed something she wasn't prepared for. A spark of something that terrified her—because there was absolutely no way she was prepared to risk her heart again.

Chapter Three

Sara drove her Jeep past the iron gates of the Elliott Ranch. She hit the horn in a double beat and waved at the new supervising foreman, Mitch Logan, who had taken over all the duties of the ranch and then some since her father's heart attack. Mitch turned from his position on the split-rail corral fence he straddled to raise a gloved hand in greeting.

Ahead at the sprawling two-story house, her father sat on a green Adirondack chair beneath the sloping eaves of the front porch. So much had changed. Last month the patriarch of Elliott Ranch could only be found on that porch when rain forced him to slow down. Now he perched on the edge of the chair, refusing to lean back and relax. A black Stetson rested on his head and hid his face as he watched the world go by, hating every minute of his forced convalescence.

Sara tried not to think about the phone call from Uncle Henry that night. Her father's heart attack was as unexpected as the Colorado storms that whipped through the valley. Before that, Hollis had convinced his daughter as well as the rest of the world that he would live forever.

Oh, yes, she should have known the hardworking, and equally hardheaded, rancher would eventually wear out the heart the good Lord had given him, but she hadn't expected it would be this soon.

Hollis Elliott was stubborn and unyielding, but he was still her father. She loved him, but could she forgive him? Could she maintain the necessary boundaries needed in order to live the life she wanted instead of the life he continued to try to orchestrate for her?

Sara pulled her Jeep into the gravel circular drive in front of the house and parked next to her father's Land Rover and their housekeeper's ancient wagon. She was anxious to get out of a dress and into boots and jeans. There was plenty of time for a long ride, and she intended to take full advantage. She missed the time away from the ranch and her horse, and wasn't ashamed to admit where her roots were. Elliott Ranch was home, and definitely her favorite place on the planet.

She approached the front porch and had barely settled her foot on the bottom step before Hollis Elliott's first directive flew.

"Stop by the dealership in Buena Vista. There's a new Land Rover with your name on it."

Taking a deep breath, she continued up the stairs. *Do not react.* Nearly twenty-four months had passed, and she liked to believe she'd learned something.

"I can't afford a new car. Besides, I love my old Jeep. It gets great gas mileage."

"That piece of tin is falling apart."

"No, it isn't. But that's beside the point. I'll decide when I need a new car."

When her father opened his mouth again, Sara reached over and kissed his leathery cheek, halting further discussion.

"Have you eaten?" she asked.

"Malla is starving me."

From the screen door, Malla Esperanza cocked her dark head to one side and clucked her tongue. "You know what they say about liars."

"Well? You call that food? A sliver of turkey and a few vegetables?"

"Your dietician calls it heart-healthy," Malla returned.

"I call it—"

"Excuse me." Sara interrupted her father's tirade.

"Can I fix you something to eat, Sara?" Malla asked, rolling her r's like a melody as she spoke.

Sara had nothing but affection for the woman who had been the sole female role model in her life since her mother died. If only she had Malla's patience and even temperament.

"No, but thank you, Malla," she said with a smile. "I ate in town. I haven't had dinner at The Prospector in years. It was delicious."

"Enough food talk," her father interrupted. "Cut to the chase. How did the meeting go?"

"It went well, Dad."

"Clinic Director. If you have to be a doctor,

then director is the way to go." His lips moved into a wistful smile. "Your mother would be proud."

"I'm auditioning for the position," Sara said. "I'll be working with another physician for eight weeks."

"What? That's a load of cow paddies." He began to stand. "Where's my phone?"

Sara touched his shoulder. "No, Dad. Stop."

Hollis sat down, grumbling. "I didn't pay for that clinic so someone else could run things."

She cocked her head. "Why did you pay for the clinic?"

"Because Henry asked me to."

"That's the only reason?"

"What are you insinuating, young lady?" His eyes narrowed in challenge.

"Nothing, but remember, your money doesn't buy you the right to manipulate other people."

Hollis released a loud snort. "We'll see about that."

Looking past her father, Sara's glance met Malla's. The older woman's eyes were wide with concern. She placed a hand on her heart in gesture and shook her head in warning, before turning away from the screen door.

Taking a deep breath, Sara relaxed and lowered her voice. "I won't stay if you interfere."

His steely black eyes met hers, but she refused to allow her gaze to waiver.

"And this time, if I leave I won't come back."

It was Hollis who finally looked away and shook his head.

Sara dug in her purse and tossed a white package with her father's blood thinner and diuretic on the small table next to him. "I picked up your scripts."

"Save your money," he grunted. I'm not taking all those pills."

"At least take the anti-cranky capsules."

He paused and blinked, then released a gruff laugh. "Very funny."

Sara placed a gentle hand upon his. "I love you, Dad, but sometimes you have to let things happen in God's timing instead of yours."

"The Lord and I have an arrangement. He runs His business and I run mine."

She couldn't contain a burst of laughter. "Not quite how it works, but nice try."

"So who is this other doctor you're up against?"

"What does it matter?" she asked.

"Invite him to the house."

Oh, that wasn't going to happen. Sara cleared her throat but was silent.

"Is that a no?" Hollis asked.

"Malla said you hired some new men to help around the ranch while you're recuperating."

"Short term. I'll be back on my feet real quick." He shook his head. "That reminds me, you have time to attend the cattlemen's meeting next week?"

"Dad, I work at the clinic. I can't help you with the ranch, too."

"Just thought I'd ask. It is your heritage."

She was silent. There was no point upsetting him. Medicine was her heritage, only he refused to acknowledge that.

"How's Mitch working out?" she countered, looking toward the corral.

"Mitch is doing just fine. No plans to court my daughter, like the last ranch manager, if that's what you mean."

She tensed and gripped her briefcase handle tightly. "That wasn't what I meant."

"Sara, you're going to have to talk about it eventually."

It? It would be the debacle that was her engagement, and he was right. She wasn't going there any time soon.

"You still blame me for that idiot fiancé of yours, don't you?" As usual, the manipulative rancher continued to prod the conversation exactly where he wanted it to go.

She sucked in a breath, determined to keep her emotions reined in. "Dad, you promised him a partnership in the ranch if we married."

"I was just encouraging things along. Nothing wrong with that."

"Except that my fiancé was in love with your offer, and not with me."

"You don't know that," her father spouted.

"But I do," she whispered, closing her eyes against the memory and the humiliation.

Hollis opened his mouth to speak and then stopped. For once he was without a sharp retort.

Sara turned and shot a forced glance toward the sky. "I'm going to change my clothes. I want to get a ride in with Rocky before the sun begins to set."

She strode into the house, stopping in the cool foyer to take several deep breaths. The tall mirror on the wall caught her reflection and Sara paused, assessing herself. Yes, she had inherited her mother's features, but was she really her mother's daughter? Her fingers moved to gently touch the trailing scar that ran along her hairline.

Amanda Elliott was an amazing doctor, loved in the community, and she had been a wonderful wife and mother, as well. She could stand up to Hollis, so why couldn't Sara?

Her mother wouldn't have run from Paradise. No, her mother never gave up on her dreams. Sara swallowed, fighting back the unexpected and overwhelming emotion. She knew she was long overdue for finding the courage to fight for those same dreams.

Dropping her briefcase in a chair, she took a deep breath and turned just as Malla came from the kitchen with the portable landline in her hand.

"Sara, are you all right?" Malla asked.

"I will be."

Malla nodded in sympathy. "The phone. It's for you," she said.

"Me? Who even knows I'm home?"

"Ben Rogers?" Malla arched a questioning brow.

"Who?"

"Dr. Ben Rogers. He is a friend of yours?"

"Ben?" Sara paused, surprised. "Yes. We work together. Thanks, Malla." Sara took the phone and moved toward the living room. "Ben. What can I do for you?"

"Sorry to bother you at home. I didn't have your cell so I thought I'd take a chance on the ranch number. I found it online."

"Really, it's all right. What's wrong?"

He cleared his throat. "I hate to impose. I mean, it is Friday night and I'm sure you have plans…"

"Yes, but Rocky is used to waiting for me. So what's up?"

"I need your skillful hands."

"Pardon me?" She blinked at his words.

"I had a little accident. Left triceps. I can't reach the area, but it looks like at least half a dozen quick sutures will close the site."

"Ben, we've got a level-four trauma center

at the Paradise E.R. Not exactly what you're used to, but they can handle this. Are you bleeding a lot? Maybe I should call 9-1-1."

"Whoa, whoa, whoa." His response was emphatic, cutting off further discussion. "Can you just bring your bag and a suture kit?" He took a deep breath. "Please."

"I'll be right over."

"Thank you." His sigh of relief was audible. "I'm at 1400 Grand Avenue. About five miles outside of town. Just stay south on Main and turn left at the dilapidated barn, then a right at the mailbox that says Miller. Oh, and don't wear your heels."

Taking the carpeted stairs two at a time, Sara grabbed her jeans from the chair she'd tossed them on this afternoon.

Despite the reason he'd called, Sara couldn't help a small frisson of pleasure that she was the one he called.

Was that a good thing? After all, she did have to work with the man for two months, and noticing that his dark eyes changed from milk chocolate to dark chocolate according to his mood or that his lips twitched attractively when he tried not to laugh or that when he said her name a shiver slid over her skin probably wasn't what Uncle Henry meant when he said they needed to get to know each other.

Besides, hadn't she learned anything in two years? If someone seemed too good to be true, they probably were. Ben Rogers would certainly prove to be no exception.

"Ouch." Ben grit his teeth as the sharp needle combined with the local anesthetic bit.

"Good grief, that was just the lidocaine," Sara said as she placed the needle on the table.

"Yeah, well, I'm generally on the other side of the injection. Guess I'll have to rethink the whole this-isn't-going-to-hurt spiel."

"If you're working as the clinic director, odds are you aren't going to have that much one-on-one patient contact."

"Okay by me."

"Is it?" Her questioning gaze met his. "I mean, are you really okay with that? I'm not so sure I am," she said.

"Sounds to me like you really don't want the director position. You're not ready to be a paper pusher. Why don't you just tell your father?"

Sara froze, her green eyes rounded. "What makes you think my father has anything to do with this?"

He narrowed his eyes but said nothing.

"Oh, I see—apparently you specialize in psychiatry in your spare time." Her jaw tensed.

"Any first-year med student could figure this out, Sara," Ben said.

She rolled back the torn edge of his starched, pinpoint-cotton dress shirt and glared at him. "Lift your arm higher."

Whoa. He'd definitely pushed a button, and she was not happy. Probably not a good idea to tick her off before she picked up a suture needle.

Ben raised his arm.

"Higher." She pulled out the suture kit, ripped open the cover and dumped the contents onto the sterile field. "Tell me again why you didn't go to the E.R. with this laceration?" Sara asked as she reassessed his arm.

"I couldn't see myself applying pressure to the site and driving at the same time."

"Hmm," was her only response.

Ben released his breath. He'd neatly side-stepped that one. No way would he step into the E.R. and then break out in a cold phobic sweat in public. His credibility would be shot to pieces, on top of the humiliation of falling and cutting his arm.

"I'm going to assume your tetanus is up-to-date."

Ben nodded.

She glanced around. "Do you have bandage scissors? Mine seem to have disappeared."

"In my bag on the couch."

Tearing off her gloves, Sara opened his satchel, then re-gloved. "Can you feel that?" she asked as she prodded his upper arm.

"Not a thing."

"Too bad," she murmured.

He nearly laughed out loud. "Doctor Elliott. What happened to *primum non nocere?*"

"Do no harm." Her lips curved into a begrudging smile, her humor apparently restored. "I'm sure Hippocrates would understand if he met you."

Ben's lips twitched. Sara Elliott was a worthy opponent. Smart, witty and beautiful. A dangerous combination under any circumstance.

Her dark lashes were lowered as she worked, and he found himself absently counting the light freckles scattered over her sun-kissed cheeks and trailing across her small upturned nose.

Minutes later she pulled off her latex gloves, and their gazes met. Sara paused, her bright eyes startled.

"What are you looking at?" she asked.

"Sixteen freckles."

"Please. Don't remind me." Annoyance laced her voice. "Those have been generously passed down from my mother's side of the family."

Ben's mind began to backtrack to Henry Rhoades's office as the light bulb slowly illuminated his thoughts. "The picture on your uncle's desk. It's you."

"Yes." The word was a soft murmur before she averted her gaze to efficiently wrap sterile gauze around his arm, trim the excess and tape the edges.

"And the woman in the picture?"

"That would be my mother, the other Dr. Elliott."

Ben swallowed, the epiphany becoming even clearer. "Your mother is Dr. Rhoades's sister."

"Correct."

All the bits of information began to fit together. *"Amanda Rhoades."*

"Yes. Amanda Rhoades-Elliott. You know who my mother is?"

"My parents spoke of her often. She was quite well known for her work in rural medicine."

"My mother was an incredible woman. Period."

"And the accident?"

"She died, and my uncle was paralyzed."

Ben stood still.

Eyes hooded, Sara began to clean up the area, carefully folding the edges of the sterile field inward until she had a neat package.

Only then did she raise her head, allowing Ben a view of the faint silvery line running close to her hairline and nearly hidden by her long hair.

"How did you get that scar?" he asked.

When she sucked in a breath and turned away, Ben's gut clenched. Why hadn't he realized it sooner?

"You were in that accident."

Sara nodded.

Suddenly things became all too clear. Her

mother died, her uncle was paralyzed and she was left with a scar to remind her of the accident for the rest of her life. Air whooshed from his lungs.

"The clinic means more than just a lot to you, Sara."

"Don't go all sentimental on me, Doc. I like you better when you're prickly." She shoved the refuse into a biohazard bag as efficiently as she had changed the subject.

Ben straightened. "I'm not prickly."

"Oh, please. I may have my issues, but so do you. You're more defensive than a momma cow." Clearing her throat, Sara glanced at his arm. "The laceration should heal nicely. Edges are well approximated. And you know the drill. Keep it clean and dry for the next forty-eight hours."

Ben nodded.

"Do you have any antibiotic ointment on hand?"

"I do."

"Great. Then you're all set." She looked around the dingy little kitchen. "Mind if I wash my hands?"

"Please." He gestured toward the old-fashioned porcelain single-basin sink.

"Tell me you called your landlord about those broken porch planks."

"Not yet. I figure we can do a little trade of services."

Sara raised her brows, blatant skepticism on her face.

"Hey, I'm handy enough around power tools. Built plenty of churches and clinics in my time. I told you my parents were medical missionaries."

Eyes narrowed, she gave him a slow assessment. "Don't take this the wrong way, but you don't exactly look like a power tool kind of guy."

Ben paused, more curious than insulted. "I don't? What kind of guy do I look like?"

"Let's just say a little more Brooks Brothers than Home Depot."

He shook his head at her assumption. "You're way off target."

Turning on the faucet, Sara's glance moved to inspect the rest of the small log cabin. "Am I? Well, by the looks of this place, that can only be a good thing."

"The Realtor called it rustic."

"Rustic?" Sara released a short laugh as she scrubbed her hands. "I'd say she saw you coming a mile away."

"Maybe so, but I don't mind. It just needs a little work."

"Good to be optimistic." She dried her hands on a paper towel.

Ben worked hard to hold back a grin as Sara continued her feisty tirade.

"I have to tell you, your three-hundred-dollar coffee machine looks a little nervous on the counter next to that kerosene lamp." She looked around again. "So what's the real reason you're out here in the middle of nowhere?"

When her probing gaze met his, he said nothing.

"Well, I suppose working with your hands is good therapy," she mused.

"You're implying I need therapy?"

"I was raised on a ranch." She shrugged. "I've been around wounded animals enough to recognize one."

"Now who's doing analysis?" he muttered.

"As you said, any first-year med student could figure it out."

"Good to know you can give as well as you get, since we'll be working together."

She snapped shut the brass latch on her leather medical bag and grabbed the handles. "And on that note, I'll be going."

"Sorry to take you away from your date."

A bright grin lit up her face. "Rocky? He's the faithful type. Always there waiting when I get home."

Ben frowned, surprised that he found himself envious. "So this is a serious relationship."

Sara laughed. "You could say that. Rocky is my horse."

"Your horse."

She only smiled.

His phone buzzed, and he pulled it from his pocket and glanced at the screen. His parents. Clamping his jaw, he took a deep breath.

"Everything okay?" Sara asked.

"Yeah. Fine."

The phone kept ringing, demanding his attention.

"Go ahead and take that," she said. "I can see myself out."

He ran a hand through his hair. "They'll call back. Let me walk you to your car."

"No need. I've got it." She stepped back, distancing herself from him, moving toward the door.

"Sara."

She turned.

"Thanks for coming all the way out here."

"No problem. Professional courtesy."

Professional courtesy? He supposed he deserved that, and yet he couldn't resist another question. "Have you considered the possibility that we could be friends?"

"Friends?" Sara cocked her head. "Are you sure? You seemed pretty adamant about the job this afternoon."

"Oh, I am adamant, but that doesn't mean we can't be friends."

"Okay, friend. So do you want me to write a script for pain medication?"

"You were going to let me suffer?"

She opened her mouth, then closed it as her cheeks flushed with color.

"I'm just giving you a hard time," he said. "I'll be fine with a little acetaminophen."

"Then I guess I'll see you Monday."

Ben nodded. Monday.

Right now Monday couldn't come soon enough. He needed to stay busy.

His phone buzzed again, just as she pushed open the rickety screen door, and he froze.

"Ben, are you *sure* everything is okay?"

"Yeah. Sure. It's all good." He nodded toward the porch. "Careful where you step."

Sara tiptoed around the broken planks and down the stairs.

When the door closed with a gentle bang, Ben slumped against the counter, unable to move as the cell phone's persistent sounds beckoned him.

Not today, Lord.

Tomorrow he'd call them. Tomorrow.

The phone kept ringing, and he continued to ignore the plea, unable to answer and hear the pain in their voices, knowing he had put it there.

His sister had gone in for a simple tonsillectomy. They'd all laughed because she'd be the oldest kid on the unit.

He'd assured his parents they didn't have to come home. Of course he'd take care of things. Except he was called away on an emergency, and when he arrived at the hospital and walked down the hall toward her room, something was very wrong.

The flurry of activity.

A code in process.

He began to run. Slamming through her doorway in time to hear the code called.

Time of death: 3:45 p.m.

Carolyn.

Ben closed his eyes tightly.

Oh, Carolyn. He'd let her down. Let them all down.

Sorry. So very sorry.

Not his fault. That's what his parents had said over and over again. But how could anyone forgive him when he couldn't forgive himself?

Chapter Four

Ben lifted his head. What was that noise? He rubbed his eyes against the morning sun that streamed into the room through the open blinds, taunting him for sleeping in. His watch showed 8:30 a.m. Something besides the twitter of birds outside his window had roused him from a deep sleep.

He'd slept solid and slept in, which hadn't happened since before… It hadn't happened in a long time.

Disoriented, he glanced around. His gaze took in the Spartan room, furnished with only a small bureau, a single chair and a small beat-up maple desk. No, this sure wasn't his lux covenant-controlled condo in Denver with its "no noise before 9 a.m." policy. Then he spotted his open suitcase in the corner. Paradise. He was in Paradise.

Perched on the edge of the mattress, he paused to listen. There it was again. Someone was at the door. How could that be? He'd rented a cabin located in a remote area five miles from town for a good reason.

Running a hand through his hair, he stepped into jeans and scooped a discarded shirt off a chair. As he shrugged into the cotton T-shirt, pain zinged through his arm. He'd forgotten about the stitches in his triceps.

Oh yeah, wide awake now.

He stumbled through the living room, nearly running into several half unpacked boxes. The place was a mess. Could he possibly get maid service in the middle of nowhere?

He opened the door and paused. The elderly man standing on the other side of the screen door grinning up at him looked familiar. A moment later, Ben made the connection. It was the gentleman who'd collapsed in the café, and he looked no worse for the trauma of yesterday's incident.

"Dr. Rogers, did we wake you?"

We? Ben glanced past the nicely dressed gentleman to see his smiling silver-haired wife peeking around her husband's shoulder.

"No. I mean, yes. I overslept." He shook his head to clear the last cobwebs. "First night in a new place. I guess I'm not used to the altitude either." Ben paused. "Can I help you, Mister, ah…"

"Carter. Orvis Carter. This is my wife, Anna."

"Morning, Doctor. Did you know you have a hole in your porch?" Perplexed, Anna Carter glanced at the splintered wood surrounding the gaping hole in his porch.

"Yes, ma'am. Found out the hard way." Ben raised his gauze-wrapped arm.

"Oh, my, my, my," Anna crooned. "Well, no worries. Our son is a carpenter. We'll have him stop by and fix that hole."

Ben narrowed his eyes, focusing on the couple. Exactly why were the Carters at his door? How had they even found his door? And why did he smell warm cinnamon?

His stomach growled loudly in hungry response. As if reading his mind, Anna stepped around her husband and thrust a large white bakery box and a thermos into his hands.

"These are yours," she said. "Our daughter-in-law Patti Jo owns the café, and she made them up special just for you. Oh, and she roasts her own coffee beans, as well. You won't taste a better cuppa than her Mountain Blend."

They'd driven all the way to the cabin on a Saturday morning just to bring him fresh pastries and hot coffee? Ben immediately regretted his cranky disposition. He paused, lacking words to respond to the unexpected kindness.

"You do like baked goods, don't you, Doc?" Orvis said, looking concerned.

"Yes. I'm a huge fan of baked goods. I eat them all the time." He shook his head. Apparently his social skills were as rusty as his bedside manner.

"I know it isn't a proper thank-you for saving my life but, well, Patti Jo does make the best cinnamon rolls in the county, and up here we take our baking pretty seriously."

"Please, tell her thank you."

"Oh, and we put some plastic bags in there,"

Anna said. "You just tuck the leftovers into the freezer. They keep for a long time."

"Thank you. So you're feeling all right?" Ben addressed Orvis. "No soreness or pain around the rib cage?"

"A bit. A bit. But only when I breathe." Orvis chuckled at his own joke. "Imagine that's to be expected."

Ben nodded. This was the strangest follow-up appointment he'd ever had. In fact, it was the first time a patient had ever made a house call. "You've got a physician who'll check you out, right?"

Orvis shook his head. "Aw, I'll be fine. Don't have much use for doctors. Present company excluded, of course." His face brightened. "Say, I hear you'll be working at the new clinic."

"That's my plan," Ben said.

"I might reconsider if you're working there." Orvis looked him up and down. "I like you, Doc. You're a man of few words. That's a rare breed around these parts."

"Thank you, Mr. Carter." Ben paused, confused by the strange compliment. "But the clinic doesn't open until late September. You need to schedule an appointment with a medical professional soon."

"Orvis. You call me Orvis." He nodded. "And I'll give it some thought."

After an awkward pause, Ben held open the door. "Would you like to come in?"

"Oh, no," Anna said. "We'll let you enjoy your Saturday."

"Sure enough, Anna is right. But we'll be back to fix that porch."

Ben worded his response carefully. "Not that I don't appreciate it, but I can probably fix those floorboards myself."

"With that arm? You go on and do your doctoring, and leave the carpentry to Orvis Jr. Our eldest really is a carpenter, you know. He's got the tools and everything." The older man moved down the stairs and walked back and forth, assessing the wide, weather-worn planks, stopping to kneel down and glance under the porch at the damaged area. "From the looks of things, this whole porch would be best replaced."

"The whole thing?"

"I dare say, Doc. The wood looks spongy, and see those struts?" He pointed to the underside of the structure. "Rotted clear through. Probably mold under there, as well. Can't believe Flora rented out the cabin in this condition."

"You know Mrs. Downey?" Ben asked.

"This is Paradise. Everyone knows Flora Downey, and it's good for business for her to know everyone."

"Whether you like it or not," Anna added.

"You know, there are plenty of nice, new rental places up by Paradise Lake. Condos and all. I'm sure Flora could fix you up."

"I'm good," Ben said. "Besides, this place is furnished."

"Furnished. You don't say," Orvis answered with a doubtful nod.

"And I was actually looking for something off the beaten track." Why did he feel the need to defend the little cabin in the middle of nowhere?

Orvis slowly glanced around at the overgrown yard and tangled shrubs that backed up to a dense forest of conifers. He raised his brows. "Guess you found it, didn't you?"

Ben returned a weak smile.

"You're a city boy." The discerning old

man wasn't asking, just stating the facts as he cocked his head, eyeing Ben up and down yet again, like he was a puzzle to be figured out.

"I'm from Denver."

"Got family there?"

"I do."

"You're a long way from home then, aren't you? All of our children are here in Paradise. Three boys and their wives. Six grandchildren." He looked hard at Ben. "Nothing as important as family."

"Uh, yes, sir."

Anna smiled. "Are you married, Dr. Rogers?"

"Me?" Ben blinked, startled at the question. "Ah, no."

"Too bad you missed our big Founder's Day Social last month, but we do have a lively singles group at church."

"I'll keep that in mind, ma'am."

"You know, Sara Elliott is single, as well," the older woman mused, assessing him with narrowed eyes. "She was engaged, but that didn't last. I daresay he broke her heart." Anna shook her head. "A shame. Sara is such a lovely girl."

Ben squirmed under her scrutiny.

"Are you matchmaking?" Orvis chided his wife.

"Why, I'm just chatting, Orvis."

"More like gossip if you ask me, and we shouldn't be gossiping about Sara. That girl's had a rough go of it."

Despite himself, Ben found himself listening closer to the banter between husband and wife once Sara's name was mentioned.

Anna turned to Orvis, a question on her face and fire in her eyes. "So when you and Orvis Jr. chaw about Hollis Elliott and how he thinks he owns Paradise because he's the richest man in these parts, is that chatting or gossiping, do you think?"

Orvis's ears reddened.

"All I'm saying is, the good Lord brought Dr. Rogers to Paradise for a reason." She smiled sweetly. "There's nothing wrong with being open to possibilities." Anna looked pointedly at Ben. "Right?"

"I, uh…" Ben stumbled over his tongue.

"Don't say anything, Doc," Orvis advised with a shake of his head, one hand raised.

"I'm telling you. Not a thing. We can't win this one."

"Yes, sir," he answered.

"I think we'd best be going now," Anna said. "Sure enjoyed chatting with you, Dr. Rogers." She shot a pointed look at her husband. "If you need anything, you just let us know."

"Just call the café," Orvis added. "Patti Jo will track us down."

"Thank you." Ben gestured awkwardly toward the box and thermos he still held cradled in one arm.

"Our pleasure," Anna said.

When the Carters' pickup truck disappeared down the dirt road, Ben turned and went into the house. He slid the box and the thermos onto the island counter and pulled open the cupboards. A couple of mugs and a few mismatched dishes would do until he could unpack his own.

He unscrewed the thermos and inhaled, wasting no time before pouring. The fresh, stout beverage was perfect, and far superior to even the pricey blend at his local coffee shop.

Impatient, he slid open the lid on the bak-

ery box. Cinnamon rolls, chocolate crois-
sants and at least a half dozen of a variety of
plump golden muffins sat between waxed tissue paper in the large box. Breakfast, lunch
and dinner, as far as he was concerned.

Warm cinnamon roll in hand, Ben headed
out the backdoor to sit on the small stoop that
faced the mountains.

Around him, birds chirped in the aspens
and tall conifers surrounding the yard. A
morning breeze wafted past, waving the
leaves of the aspen like green coins and bringing in the scents of summer. Honeysuckle,
grass and a hint of pine.

Yeah, Paradise all right. He bit into the
pastry and paused mid chew. No wonder the
customers were lined up in the café. Slowly
savoring the roll, he analyzed the unkempt
yard, mentally adding lawn mower to his
shopping list. A hammock would be good,
too, and a barbecue grill.

Maybe he could get them in Paradise and
avoid driving into Monte Vista. He'd seen a
grocery and a hardware store in town.

Leaning back, Ben sighed.

This was nice. Real nice.

Nicer than he deserved.

A man could forget his troubles in a setting like this. Like a wound that hadn't been treated, the problem with ignoring your troubles was that it didn't actually make them go away.

No, he'd learned the hard way, after sitting in a dark apartment for six months, that they refused to go away until you dealt with them.

"Ben?"

Sara pushed her grocery cart down the aisle, closer to the towering display of cereal boxes. "What are you doing?"

"Grocery shopping." He tugged at the bill of his cap and adjusted his dark sunglasses.

"Where's your cart?"

"Oh, it's parked around here somewhere. I think." He glanced around, looking more and more distracted by the second.

When he shoved his hands into his pockets, Sara noted the white gauze peeking out from his short-sleeved shirt.

"How's your arm?"

"A nuisance, but fine. Thanks again for coming out last night." He raised his head and peered over his shoulder at the front of the store, before stepping farther back behind the giant cardboard cutout of a bowl and milk.

His behavior was nothing short of bizarre, and she couldn't help but ask, "Are you hiding from someone?"

Ben swallowed, then turned and tilted his head toward the checkout lanes.

Bewildered, Sara followed his gaze to where three silver-haired women stood chatting. "What am I looking at?"

"Those women. See the tall one with the bun on the top of her head? She appears to be the ringleader."

"You're hiding from the Paradise Ladies' Auxiliary?"

His brows shot up from behind the shades. "You know them?"

"Yes. They just happen to be part of a very nice group of Christian women who do community service for Paradise."

"They're stalking me."

Sara's eyes widened, and she bit back a laugh.

"Stalking. Like gang activity or something?"

"You don't believe me."

"I didn't say that, but you're giving me a

visual of the women of the Paradise Ladies' Auxiliary riding through town on motorcycles terrorizing the town."

He glared at her. "Why do I think you aren't taking me seriously?"

"Because I've known those women all my life, and they're harmless. I think we can probably chalk this up to a miscommunication."

"Miscommication? By whom?" He raised a brow. "First I was cornered in the hardware store. A twenty-minute lecture on the flora indigenous to the area ensued. They offered to assist with yard maintenance. I politely declined. Then I stopped by the café for a coffee, and they pulled up chairs at my table for another chat, this time about delivering hot meals to my house while my arm heals. Again, I politely declined. Now I'm grocery shopping, and they show up." Both brows were raised as he stared pointedly at her. "Still going with the miscommunication theory?"

"No, now I'm going with small-town neighborliness."

"Sara, they also mentioned a single granddaughter I should meet."

Sara put a hand over her mouth.

Ben frowned. "Something funny?"

"Yes. You."

"Sure, funny to you. You aren't the object of their attention."

"Well, let me ask you this. Would it hurt to let them bring hot meals to the cabin?"

He pulled off his glasses and pinned her with his dark eyes. "Here's the thing. I like being alone. In fact, I'm not a real social being."

She feigned a gasp. *"No. Really? You?"*

He glared.

"How did they find out about your arm?" she asked.

"Anna Carter would be my guess."

"How did Anna Carter find out about your arm?"

"Anna and Orvis came out to the cabin this morning."

"If you hadn't saved Orvis's life and become a town hero, none of this would have happened."

Ben snorted. "So this is my fault?"

"Look, you're in Paradise, Colorado, population—"

"Seventeen-hundred and eighteen," he recited.

"I'm concerned you know that." She shook

her head and continued. "The number of single men under the age of sixty-five in this town is only slightly higher than the number of sightings of the Paradise Lake Monster."

"There's a Paradise Lake Monster?"

She raised her brows. "Ben, it's a myth. Relax. What I'm trying to say is that if you're going to survive Paradise, you've got to chill. This isn't the big city. People talk to you on the street here, drop by unannounced, and sometimes they even ask how your kids are."

"I don't have kids."

"Yes, but you do happen to be the most exciting news that's blown into town in a while. Maybe you could find a way to use that to your advantage."

He pulled off his cap, then slapped it back on. "That's all the advice you can offer?"

"Advice?" She gripped the grocery cart. "Hmm, well, I can suggest you plan your outings for Wednesday evenings from now on."

"I'm afraid to ask why."

"That's when the Paradise Ladies' Auxiliary meets at Bitsy's house."

"Don't think I don't appreciate the insider information, but what do I do in the meantime?" he asked.

Sara looked him up and down, knowing she was going to regret what she was about to say. "I suppose I could help you out."

"You'd do that?" He perked up.

"Of course you'll owe me," she said, her lips curving into a smile.

"Anything."

"Oh, that's a given."

Ben paused and raised his brows at her comment. "So what's the plan?" he asked.

"I'll have to give them someone or something else to save. And that," she sighed, "won't be easy."

"I'm not sure I follow."

"The Ladies' Auxiliary needs a mission. Right now, you're it." Sara glanced around. "Until I find an alternate project for them, you'd better slip out the service door." She nodded toward the back of the store.

"How do you know where the service door is?"

"I used to work here."

Ben's face reflected his surprise. "Dr. Sara Elliott worked at the Pay and Sack?"

"You bet, and I was the top cashier for three

years running." She glanced at Ben. "You can close your mouth now."

"I'm sorry. I just…"

"What?"

"Nothing," he said.

"I'll have you know I worked at the Pay and Sack every summer through high school and college."

"Why?"

"Because I needed to know I could do it myself. Ever since the accident, my father has tried to put me in a bubble to protect me."

"And you've fought him every step of the way," he returned.

Sara met his gaze head-on. The man had pieced together just enough to be dangerous.

"Okay," she said. "Therapy session is over. Besides, Bitsy's headed this way. Go down the stairs. Follow the restroom sign. Last door on your left. Make sure the lock catches behind you."

"Thanks, Sara."

"Don't thank me. You aren't off the hook yet. We've still got to find something to keep the ladies busy and their focus off you."

"We?" Ben turned slightly and looked at her as he headed down the steps.

"For now, we're in this together," she said.

"Coconspirators." Ben grinned.

Sara wasn't smiling as she watched him disappear from view. Ben Rogers was quickly becoming more and more involved in her life, and that couldn't possibly be a good thing. He'd managed to analyze her at every turn without sharing much of anything about himself. It was definitely time to turn the tables on the good doctor.

Chapter Five

Ben inserted his key in the lock of the outside door of the clinic before he realized it was already open. He pushed on the metal bar as he glanced at his watch. Seven o'clock. According to Dr. Rhoades, the contractors wouldn't show until nine. The only other keys to the facility belonged to Sara and her uncle. He turned back to check out the parking lot again, but there were no cars.

In the empty lobby of the clinic, a mountain bike was propped against boxes of shelving units and a stack of carpet tiles. A blue helmet dangled from the bike's handlebars. Ben inspected the bike. It wasn't just a bicycle, it was a serious mountain bike complete with gadgets he couldn't even identify.

He moved down a newly carpeted hall, where the smell of carpet glue, fresh paint and coffee permeated the air. At the first lit office doorway, he peered in. Sara Elliott sat on the floor with a tower of manila file folders in front of her. Her dark hair hung like a curtain, shielding her face as she studied the open folder in her lap with intensity.

Ben found himself staring for a moment. Was Sara as uncomplicated as she seemed? For all that she'd been through, she ought to be an emotional mess, yet she always appeared happy and upbeat. Her infamous father seemed to be the only bump in her road.

He was used to people with agendas. She didn't seem to have one, and that made him nervous.

What bothered him most of all was that he couldn't deny that he was drawn to her. That wasn't good either, because unlike Sara, he was a myriad of doubts and emotional question marks.

She looked up and a smile lit her lips, reaching and igniting the sparkle in her eyes.

How could it be that one small smile could

warm the cold emptiness within him? Ben swallowed hard, fighting the connection she offered.

"You're here early," Sara said. "I'm sure Dr. Rhoades will be impressed."

"I wasn't exactly looking to impress him."

She arched a brow. "No?"

"No. And I hate to point out the obvious, but you beat me in."

"I was going stir-crazy at the ranch." She shrugged. "What's your excuse?"

"Pretty much the same thing. I've been out of the game for the last six months. Now all I want to do is get to work."

"What have you been doing for the last six months?" she asked.

"That's a long, boring story." He paused. "Is that your bike in the lobby?"

Sara nodded. "My car is in the shop for maintenance—having its rubber bands changed."

"Excuse me?"

"Inside joke." Amusement touched her lips. "My father says my car is held together with rubber bands. He wants to buy me a new expensive model, like your toy."

"And you refused."

"Because I don't need a new car."

"You've heard the term pick your battles?" he asked.

"Yes, thank you, Sigmund."

As the warning lights flashed, Ben stepped back from the landmine, quickly changing the subject. "So, do you ride the bike a lot?"

She grinned, and her expression said she hadn't missed his careful retreat. "Not as much since I left Paradise. There's nothing like a morning bike ride through the valley to make you appreciate life."

"That's quite a bike."

"Bikes are serious business around here. If you're going to ride, you have to have one that won't let you down on the trail."

"Maybe I should get a bike," Ben said. "Would you mind if I tag along sometime?"

Her eyes narrowed. "Really?"

"Why is that so surprising?"

"I didn't take you for the jock type." She cocked her head, assessing him once again.

"Haven't we had this discussion before?"

"Yes, and I'm still trying to figure out what someone like you is doing in Paradise."

"Someone like me."

"Uh-huh. Do you know how hard it is to retain physicians out here?"

"Is that a rhetorical question?"

She kept talking, all the while assessing him. "You could be living the cush life, as a big-city hospitalist, with ten days on and seven days off. Outrageous salary. Social contacts." She chewed on the end of her pen. "In fact, I'd bet that's exactly where you came from." Sara paused. "So, why Paradise? The clinic director position certainly won't keep you in the financial or social style you're accustomed to."

"Is that a no on the bike ride?"

Her eyes widened for a moment before she burst out laughing. "I'll be happy to show you around the trails in Paradise, Dr. Rogers. But be forewarned, I'm determined to figure you out."

"Sorry, Sara, but you're overthinking this. There is nothing to figure out."

"Uh-huh," she murmured.

Ben glanced around. "Any idea when the furniture is supposed to arrive?"

She shook her head. "No, but I imagine

we could borrow some folding tables from the hospital."

"Good idea. Want to call your uncle?"

"He should be here soon." She looked him up and down. "So you're feeling okay?"

"Yeah." He rotated his arm. "I might have overdone it doing yard work, but the last time I checked, both the incision and my yard looked really good."

"I wasn't talking about your arm, or your yard. You seemed awfully pale yesterday at orientation, and then you disappeared after the tour."

"Something I ate maybe? Anyhow, I'm fine now." He sniffed the air. "Do I smell coffee?"

"Follow me." Sara picked up her cup and led him into a small kitchenette, where she pulled open a cupboard. "The drug reps have been here already. You can have your choice. Check out the black-and-gold anti-fungal mug. Then there's the friendly 'statin of the month' cup. Or…" She waved a hand in the air like a game show hostess. "The amazing stainless-steel benzodiazepine travel mug."

"Decisions, decisions." Ben grabbed the

travel mug and turned. "Whoa. That's a lot of pastries."

"No kidding," Sara said.

He reached for the carafe of coffee. "You brought four boxes of pastries on your bike?"

"They were delivered from Patti Jo's. Know anything about that?"

"Who me?" His gaze met hers, and suddenly the penny dropped into the slot. "The Carters?"

"Bingo."

He shrugged. "I'm sure the contractors will be very happy. Oh, and I can recommend the pecan praline muffins."

"Ditto. I've already had one. Better carb up yourself. You're going to need the energy. We've got a lot of resumes and CVs to go through."

"Oh?" He followed her back to the office.

Sara retrieved two stacks of folders from the piles on the floor. "Pick one."

"What am I picking?"

"Staff you get to interview. Which brings us back to the topic of physicians. I'm praying we can bring two physicians on board well before September, but I don't have a clue how to attract them to a position with a non-competitive salary in the middle of, well…" She laughed. "Paradise."

He raised his brows at her pun and grabbed the left pile to begin reviewing the tabs. "You and I were interested in relocating to Paradise."

"We aren't the norm."

Their eyes met, and Ben released a small chuckle.

"You know what I mean," Sara returned.

"I do, and that's a little scary."

She smiled. "Anyhow, I'm hoping we can get through all these files by Friday. Think you can do it?"

"You like to keep everything competitive, don't you?" Ben commented.

"Absolutely," she agreed. "But usually I only have myself to compete with. I have to admit that this is much more fun."

Ben nearly laughed aloud.

"Oh, and did you look at the purchasing plan they gave us?" she asked.

"Yeah, last night. That plus the policy-and-procedure manual from the hospital put me right to sleep."

"I think that was the goal." She grinned.

"Genius." He nodded and sipped his coffee.

"Apparently someone from the hospital is coming over to look at the exam rooms and order big-ticket items along with the large inventory, including computers and printers. We'll just have to review their purchase order."

"Okay, and what about office supplies and paper products, forms and vendors?" Ben asked.

"My thought was that if we hire an office manager right away, we get out of counting paper clips."

Ben gave her a thumbs-up. "Let's do it."

"Take a look at the top file. She's my choice."

"Mind if I pull up a spot on the floor with you?" he asked.

"Be my guest."

They worked quietly in comfortable silence for over an hour until Sara's phone began to buzz in her briefcase. "Would you excuse me?"

"Sure."

When she left the room, Ben stood and

stretched his legs. Grabbing his coffee, he wandered down the hall past the front desk to the other hallway. Turning right, he discovered another door that opened to a large yard. Concrete walkways had been poured and the soil turned over, but that's where the landscaping ended. No trees or plants of any kind. Nothing but six-foot-tall cedar fencing.

The sun was just above the tree line, and he could see clear to the snowcapped mountains. He stared, mesmerized by the beautiful scenery before him. Every day it seemed there was something that caused him to pause and consider that God had touched the tiny town of Paradise.

"Spectacular view, isn't it?"

Ben turned to see the hospital medical director behind him, approaching in his wheelchair.

"Dr. Rhoades. Good morning, sir. What is this place?"

"This is supposed to be the clinic gardens. I envisioned an area for meditation with a reflection pond, maybe a fountain and a small gazebo. I hoped we could use the area for receptions, possibly even weddings. But unfortunately, the funding isn't there. So it may just end up as a patch of grass."

"A patch of grass with an amazing view."

Henry smiled. "Yes. That it is." He turned, and his probing eyes assessed Ben. "Are you feeling all right? Keeping hydrated? I thought you might have a bit of altitude sickness yesterday during our hospital tour."

"I'm feeling fine, sir. Thanks for asking."

Henry nodded thoughtfully. "So, have you seen the chapel?"

"No, sir, I haven't."

"You went out the wrong door. Follow me."

Ben walked behind the wheelchair, across a stamped cement patio to a set of double doors. Dr. Rhoades pressed the automatic button, and the doors slowly and silently swung open. They moved inside the building to a dark room.

"On the wall to your left. Hit that light switch."

Ben did, and the room came alive.

An organ took up most of the front, then rows of polished oak pews filled the rest of the room. A single wooden cross adorned the wall in the small sanctuary illuminated by soft recessed lighting.

Henry gestured with his hands. "The wood in that paneling and those benches is from local trees. See that marble in the sanctuary altar? From Marble, Colorado. It's the same white marble that's used for the Tomb of the Unknown Soldier in Washington, D.C. The slab was given to us by a hospital patron."

For a long moment, both men were silent.

"I feel the Lord's presence in this room already," the older man said.

"Yes." Ben nodded. Dr. Rhoades was right; there was something tranquil and comforting about the room.

"I wanted a place that would honor the Lord because He planted the seed for the clinic in my sister's heart."

"I admire you, Dr. Rhoades. You've turned an unfortunate incident into a positive one, and are making a difference because of it."

Henry narrowed his eyes. "Is that how it appears?"

Ben opened his mouth and closed it, not sure what the correct response would be, but feeling fairly confident he'd already said the wrong thing.

"Your words are very generous, son, but if you're going to be a part of the clinic's future, you must understand the vision."

Ben swallowed.

"The residents of this area, as well as our transient tourist population, have long needed a responsive medical facility. Not just any clinic, but one staffed with medical person-nel who are willing to go to them when they can't come to us."

"Yes, sir."

"*That* was my sister's dream. It was only too ironic that she died because medical help couldn't reach her."

Ben nodded slowly.

"What I want from a director is someone who can not only do the job, but understands the community we are serving and is willing to think outside the box to get the job done and meet those needs. Someone who will do everything in his power for Paradise."

Ben cleared his throat. "Sir, have I offended you?"

"No." Henry Rhoades shook his head and

pressed his lips together, pausing for a moment. "Forgive me, but you gave me a reality check, son. I've been so excited about the clinic that I think I forgot what really matters."

He wheeled his chair around, glancing at the room as he moved. "The clinic is not a trophy, or a monument to anything we've done. In fact, it's not about you or me or Sara or Hollis." His gaze focused upon the wooden cross. "It's about the vision the Lord gave my sister. I've got to trust that somehow, that vision will be fulfilled completely." He looked at Ben. "Our job is simply to do His will."

"Ben?" Sara rounded the corner, looking for him.

His hands reached for her shoulders before they collided.

"Sorry," she mumbled, moving out of his arms. Pink flooded her face, and she glanced away for a moment. "I was just looking for you. Did you get lost?"

"Had to stretch my legs. Sitting on the floor isn't as easy as it used to be." When he looked at her, he knew something was wrong. The bright green eyes were now dark with worry.

"What's up?" he asked.

She seemed to struggle with a response, finally taking a deep breath before her words came out in a rush. "The Boulder Clinic called."

"Your previous job."

"Technically, I'm still employed there."

"Oh?" Startled, he turned to look at her again as they headed down the corridor of offices. "I didn't realize."

"Yes, and to further complicate things, I was just offered the director position."

Ben narrowed his eyes. "And you're telling me this because…?"

Sara stopped in the middle of the hall. Hands on her hips, she huffed. "Because we're working together, and I want to be upfront with you."

"Hey, no need to get annoyed. I'm just asking."

"I'm not annoyed."

"Right."

She clenched and unclenched her hands. "I am not annoyed. I'm confused. I get cranky when I'm confused."

"I'll try not to confuse you," Ben murmured.

"Thank you."

"So what are you going to tell them?"

"I don't know," she groaned. "They've given me until the end of August to decide. Then they turn it over to the head hunters."

"So you've got your foot in the door to both clinics? Sort of a safety net?" Ben shook his head and headed to the kitchen. Sara was right behind him.

"It sounds terrible when you say it like that."

He looked at her, but said nothing as he poured coffee into his cup.

"Look, I love Paradise, but I'm just not sure I can handle my father. It's a double-edged sword. I'd like to stay. He's not well. But he continues to interfere in my life, and my career. The funny thing is, I'm pretty sure he thinks this doctor thing is a phase, and I'll come to my senses and take an interest in running the ranch." She sighed, and her eyes continued to plead with him for an answer.

"You know," Ben said, "when I have tough decisions to make, I have a plan for strategizing."

"Oh?"

He nodded. "I take a legal pad and write down the pros and cons in two separate columns. Then tear the paper off, throw it in the trash and go pray."

Sara paused, then blinked. Her lips curved into a smile, and she started to laugh.

"Hey, I was serious," he said.

"I know. The irony of the situation is that I just handed you the opportunity to push me out the door to Boulder," Sara responded.

Ben frowned.

"And you didn't."

"What was I thinking?" Ben raised a palm.

When she looked up at him, green eyes earnest, Ben fought the urge to smooth a tangled tendril of dark hair that had fallen across her cheek. He paused. It was the first time he'd seen her vulnerable, and he found himself wanting to make things all better.

Crazy. He'd known her less than a week. She was right—he should be pushing her out the door to Boulder. The woman was dangerous to the very peace he was searching for.

"Look, Sara, in the end you just have to do what's right for you. I'm thinking you already know that." He sipped his coffee.

"I'm also concerned that you haven't tried to psychoanalyze me and blame it all on my relationship with my father."

He couldn't resist a grin.

She sighed and kept talking, not waiting for a response. "Well, this isn't going to be easy. There are a lot of great things about Boulder."

"Such as?"

"There's the free clinic. I helped launch the program. They said it couldn't be done, but we did it. It's been an incredible community outreach."

"You did it once. You could do it again here in Paradise."

"It's taken years to get funding for this clinic alone. What makes you think I can get pledges for funding to support free medical care?"

"This clinic didn't have you in the equation until now."

Her eyes widened, and she smiled. "Good answer."

"I meant it. And I was just talking to your uncle. He said we should think outside the box. In fact, he really challenged me to consider exactly what this community needs from this clinic."

"It's all in the paperwork," Sara said.

"Seeing it on paper isn't the same as seeing it with my eyes. How can I understand what the community needs if I don't even know the community?"

"Road trip," Sara announced, her voice enthusiastic. "How about a little tour of the valley and the foothills?"

Ben nodded. "That would be great."

Sara's eyes sparkled. "Do you have plans for Saturday?"

"Saturday works for me."

"Your car or mine?" he asked.

"Yours. My Jeep is a little pedestrian for your tastes."

"Excuse me?"

"Sorry. Sorry." She raised her hands. I'm trying very hard not to judge the doctor by the price of his stethoscope."

"My stethoscope?" Ben choked out the words.

"I couldn't help but notice that you have one of those high-end, five-hundred-dollar electronic Littmanns. I bet you can hear crepitus in the next room with that thing."

"Jealous?" He laughed.

"You bet I am," Sara said.

"It was a graduation present from my sister."

"Nice sister."

"Finally, something we can agree on." He cocked his head and looked at her. "Are you aware that while you are the daughter of the richest man in the area, you've got some kind of prejudice against rich people?"

"Do I?" She frowned, her brow wrinkling in thought. "I don't think anyone's ever pointed that out to me before."

"They don't dare. Your father is the Cattle King of Paradise Valley."

"I'll take your interesting diagnosis under consideration, but I'd like to point out that you've got some overcompensation issues going on yourself, Doctor."

Ben couldn't resist laughing. "So I'll drive tomorrow?"

"What is it you drive, anyhow?"

"Land Rover," he mumbled.

"You aren't serious?" She shook her head.

"What?"

"That would be the same vehicle the Cattle King of Paradise Valley drives. I can't believe I didn't notice it the other night."

"What can I say? Your father has good taste." He shrugged. "So I'm still driving?"

Sara shook her head. "If you insist."

Ben smiled. Sara Elliott was challenging, interesting and frustrating. It seemed she could never be boring. Sara was fun, and he hadn't felt this good in a very long time.

Chapter Six

It was just before eight when Ben drove the Land Rover into the parking lot of the clinic. Naturally Sara was already there and waiting. He shook his head. Somehow she'd managed to beat him to the clinic every day this week, and leave after he did. Oh yeah, Sara was definitely giving him a run for his money. She was bringing out his old competitive edge, and he wasn't sure yet if that was a good thing.

She sat on the hood of her car in cargo pants, a red pullover and hiking books, her hair in a low ponytail. He chuckled. Sara didn't look anything like his starchy colleagues back in Denver. Although she was definitely easier on the eyes, his life would probably be a lot simpler if she didn't look so cute.

"Good morning." Sara shot him a grin and hopped off the car, her ponytail flipping into the air with the action. She reached into the backseat of her ancient Jeep and tugged until finally a very large, canvas duffel bag popped out, propelling her backwards.

Ben leaped forward and grabbed her wrist, pulling her upright inches before her backside hit the pavement. "You brought your suitcase?" he asked.

"Supplies." She glanced at his hand, which still held her by the wrist, and smiled. "Thank you."

Ben let go, with the odd realization that this was the second time he'd caught Sara before she fell, and he really liked holding on to her. "No problem," he murmured.

"I've learned never to spend the day driving through the valley and the mountains without being prepared."

Groaning, he heaved up the duffel and headed to his car. "This thing weighs a ton. What did you pack?"

"The usual. Water. Granola bars. Sunscreen.

Road flares. Flashlight. Plastic trash bags. A compass. First-aid kit. Matches. Duct tape. Oh, and a coat, and a change of clothes."

Stunned, he simply stared.

"Up here, supplies can be the difference between life and death." She grinned. "And no worries. I brought extra for you."

Well, she was the expert, he'd give her that. "So do you get a lot of medical emergencies in the mountains during the summer?" Ben asked.

"In a word? Yes. During the summer there are amateur bicyclists, rafters, hikers, campers, bird watchers and photographers all pitted against Mother Nature. Mother Nature generally wins."

"Hadn't considered that. But aren't there, like, forest rangers to help?"

"Are you serious? This is the edge of the Rio Grande National Forest. It's the largest alpine valley in the world. The rangers do a huge amount of conservation education besides monitoring something like over a million acres of land. They have plenty to do besides first aid."

"Whoa. I guess so." He opened the back

of the Land Rover, shoved in the duffel and was preparing to close it when she called out.

"Hang on. I want to get the sleeping bag from the front seat."

"Sleeping bag? Now we're camping?"

"Just a precaution, Ben. Once we leave the city limits, cell phone service is pretty much nonexistent. You just never know." She tossed the roll toward him.

"Apparently not," he said as he caught the nylon sack.

"Do much hiking?" Sara asked. She pulled a tube of sunscreen from one of her roomy cargo pants pockets and slathered it on her arms and face.

"Hiking? Why?"

"Just thinking about our itinerary." She capped the bottle and handed it to him.

"I walk from the gym to my car." He shrugged. "Does that count?"

"Don't worry. I'll take it easy on you today."

Ben patted his abdomen through his shirt. "I'm not exactly out of shape."

Sara chuckled. "I wasn't trying to emasculate you. Climbing and hiking in this altitude takes some adjustment. I'm suggesting we take it slow. We'll do more next time."

"Next time?" Ben asked. He lifted his brows.

"I consider it my duty to make you as familiar with these back roads and hills as I am."

"I thought this was a driving tour." Now he was getting worried. He wasn't prepared to perform.

"It is, but we have to be prepared. You never know when the weather will change up here. Thunderstorms. Hail. Flash flooding. Oh, and I want to show you a few things off the beaten path." She wagged a finger. "And that, my supposedly fit friend, will require walking."

"Don't worry, I'm fit enough for that," Ben said, relieved.

"So you like outdoor recreation?" Sara asked.

"In small doses. I grew up camping. I like things a little more civilized now. But let me guess. You like activities that are measurable."

"Measurable?" Sara cocked her head.

"Yeah, where you can measure yourself against something."

"How did you guess?"

"My sister was like that," Ben said. "In fact, she had to stop wearing a watch when she went running because she kept timing herself and discovered she was no longer enjoying the beauty of the run."

"Oh, I can so relate," Sara said with a laugh.

"You're a lot like her," Ben mused. "Carolyn used to beg me to run with her just for the satisfaction of beating me. And she did. Every time."

He paused, staring out the windshield, stunned to discover he'd just talked about his sister. For the first time since her death, he was able to just think about the good times without being chased down by the agonizing guilt.

"I think I'd like your sister."

Ben looked at Sara. "Yeah. You would."

Sara and Carolyn could have easily become friends. They both had the same sense of humor and optimistic outlook, along with the same stubbornness and competitive streaks.

The thought made him smile.

* * *

"Lots of tourists," Ben commented, as another vehicle with out-of-state tags zipped past them.

Sara turned in her seat. His baseball cap was slightly skewed and his expensive sunglasses were dusty. Yet despite himself, she could tell Ben was having fun today. He'd stopped trying to hide it about an hour ago at the last parking turnout when she'd forced him to pose for pictures. She didn't know why, but there was immense pleasure involved in helping the stuffy Dr. Ben Rogers chill out.

"The population around here quadruples to over four thousand visitors during camping season," she told him. "Thankfully that's a small window—between May and the end of September."

"Well, that would explain all the RVs."

"Uh-huh. And that window is just long enough to keep things really busy at the Paradise E.R."

"Which is a good reason for the clinic to have a twenty-four-hour urgent care," he added.

"Yes. Along with our one-day-a-month free

clinic," Sara said, unable to hold back her excitement. She pulled a notebook out of her purse. "I'm writing all this down."

"Don't forget to document that I hiked from that point of interest to the top of the trail," Ben said.

"I was talking about the clinic, but I'll be sure to add you to my list." Sara laughed. "It was worth it, wasn't it? The view was amazing."

"Amazing, definitely. But you're right. My lungs aren't acclimated enough for a hike at ten thousand feet. I should have brought my O2 tank with me."

"You'll be in shape in no time."

There was a long pause as the unsaid words drifted between them like a ribbon of smoke silently dangerous and threatening. *In no time.* The same no time it would take for the clinic to open and for one of them to get the job. And the other?

Sara pushed the thoughts out of her mind. No, she didn't want to think about that right now. She liked Ben, and she was glad for this opportunity to get to know him better. She didn't want to wish the time with him away—

no, she definitely intended to savor the time, because as much as it seemed they had some basic philosophical differences, she was discovering they also had a lot in common.

"Do you want me to drive?" she asked.

Ben looked at her and frowned. "You can't diss the car and then ask to drive it."

"Fine." She rolled her eyes. "But let's take a lunch break soon. I'm starving."

"You packed lunch?"

"Just a few sandwiches and apples. They're in the duffel." Another RV passed them, and Sara looked pointedly at the speedometer. "It's okay to go faster."

Ben's brows shot up above his sunglasses. "You think I'm driving too slow?"

"The term little old lady did come to mind, especially when we hit all those switchbacks."

His jaw dropped in obvious indignation. "Seriously?"

Sara lifted a shoulder. "What can I say? I know the mountains so I drive a little more, shall we say, confidently."

He shook his head and mumbled, "Tell me how you really feel."

Eyes on the road, Sara smiled as she read the mile marker. "We're almost there. After the next bend, there's a spot about a half mile down the road. There." She pointed, excitement bubbling up inside. "See that parking area?"

"Got it." Ben slid the car into the parking area.

Shivers of anticipation danced over her skin as she burst from the car and jogged the several hundred yards to a railing that overlooked a drop-off.

An endless blanket of wildflowers was spread before her. Blossoms of red, blue, yellow and purple danced in the gentle breeze. The field was punctuated with more boulders than she remembered. But they had probably rolled down the mountain during the spring runoff. Farther away, a small stream ran through the rocks.

She hadn't been back here in two years. Yet nothing had really changed. *Thank You, Lord, for that.* She needed this part of her world to stand still. "I take it you know this place," Ben said moments later from behind her.

She nodded.

"Just look at those wildflowers," he said.

"My mother loved them."

"Do you know what they are?"

"Of course." She began to identify them: "Indian paintbrush, columbine, lupine and fireweed. Next to the stream are primroses."

He turned to the metal plate attached to the railing, then removed his sunglasses before he read the words aloud. "In loving memory of Amanda Rhoades-Elliott." Pausing, Ben raised his head and met Sara's gaze. His face was stark, and his eyes brimmed with concern.

"This is where the accident was," he said.

"Yes."

Ben rubbed a hand over his face before speaking again. "It doesn't upset you to come back here?"

"No. In my heart, this is where my mother lives. So when I come back here, to the mountains she loved, it's as though I regain my direction. This place is my compass." She inhaled deeply.

Sara could feel the intensity of Ben's gaze as he silently searched for something in her response. "Would you like to be alone?" he finally asked.

"Ben, really, I'm fine. I chose to come back here."

Past the field the sky was a cloudless bright

blue, providing a canvas for rows of conifers in the distance and the majestic capped peaks beyond. "How could anyone look at that and doubt there is a God?" she mused.

"I don't know," Ben said. He was silent for several minutes before finally asking, "Can you tell me about it?"

"The accident?"

"Yeah," he murmured.

"Honestly, I don't remember that much. Most of it my uncle told me afterwards. I do remember that I was in the backseat. Reading as usual. My mother was driving. It was snowing, but I don't recall that conditions were unusually severe. Suddenly the car lurched. We hit a patch of ice. My mother lost control of the vehicle, and it rolled over several times and ended up in that clearing." She pointed to the field before them.

"Over the rail and embankment?" Ben's eyes were wide.

"Both the rail and the embankment buildup were added after the accident. We've driven through the mountains all day, Ben. This is hardly a dangerous spot compared to the cliffs and drop-offs we've seen. But my father pressured the county to add those."

Ben gave a short nod as Sara continued.

"Apparently my uncle had taken off his seat belt for a moment to reach for some papers in the back. He was thrown from the car. My mother died on impact. I was pinned in the car for hours."

"Your scar?"

She touched her face, her fingertips gingerly traversing the familiar disfigurement. "The car rolled into a boulder, smashing in the passenger side and jutting through the window, cutting my face and trapping me inside. Looking back, I was probably concussed, which explains why I don't remember much."

With a grimace, Ben closed his eyes and swallowed. When he finally opened them, he stared out at the field, his face an angry mask.

Without thinking, Sara reached out and wrapped her arms around him. Holding tightly, she rested her head against his chest for a minute, listening to the beat of his heart. A strong, steady heart. It took an effort to step away from him.

She hadn't figured Ben Rogers out yet, but something kept whispering to her that he needed Paradise far more than he let on. What was he holding so tightly inside of him? Whatever it was, one thing was clear: today he needed a hug far more than she did.

"What was that for?" Ben asked, his dark eyes wide with surprise.

"I'm not sure." Sara released a small smile. She should be embarrassed, but oddly enough, she wasn't. "You looked like you needed a hug."

"Maybe I did," he acknowledged quietly. "I don't know how you handle it so well."

"My mother's death?"

"That, and the unfairness of it all." He shook his head. Bitterness shadowed his face. "We spend our lives saving people, and yet there is so much out of our control."

"You're right, of course. But I choose to look at what I can control instead of what I can't." She paused and cleared her throat as emotions threatened. "I've had a lifetime to deal with my loss. Lots of time for denial, anger, self-recrimination."

"How could you possibly blame yourself?" Ben asked.

"When you're going through the grief process, playing 'what if' and faulting yourself doesn't have to make sense. In fact, it probably never does."

Ben stiffened as he stared out at the mountains in the distance.

"Not a day goes by that I don't think of her," she continued. "I miss her. She believed in me. Not in what I could be, but she believed in me just for who I was. That's the legacy my mother left me."

Sara slowly ran her palm over the dull metal plaque. Less than ten words that marked the moment her life changed forever.

"For me," she continued, "it all comes down to one question. Am I going to hold out my hand and trust the Lord even though life isn't fair, even though I have more questions than answers?"

Ben's searching gaze met hers, and she again glimpsed the tortured pain in the depths of the dark eyes as he silently pleaded for something. Something she didn't know how to give him.

"The answer will always be yes, Ben. *Trust in the Lord with all your heart and lean not unto your own understanding. In all your ways acknowledge Him, and He will direct your paths.*" She exhaled. "It's not an option."

His eyes became glassy with emotion, and he looked away. In that moment Sara knew. Ben Rogers understood her loss because he'd been there. He'd been to the bottom of the despair and was still fighting his way out of the abyss.

She reached out and touched his hand. "Oh, Ben. I'm so sorry. But it will get better. I promise."

"Will it? You seem to have it all figured out," Ben said, his gaze never leaving the scenery before them. "But maybe…maybe I don't deserve better."

Sara inhaled sharply. "How can you say that?"

"You don't know the situation, Sara."

"No, I guess I don't." She acknowledged his words, her hand dropping back to her side. "But the Lord does. And you've got to let someone in. Why not Him?"

Chapter Seven

Ben snuck another glance at Sara as he drove. They'd barely spoken, both lost in their own thoughts for the past hour since leaving the site of that long-ago accident.

"Don't miss that turn up ahead." Sara's voice interrupted his thoughts.

"What? Sorry. I wasn't paying attention." Ben navigated the car onto a two-lane road.

Suddenly she shot straight up in the passenger seat. "Ben, pull over."

"Why?"

"There's a motorcycle down. You have to pull over." Her voice was tense and tight.

He yanked off his sunglasses. "Where?"

"See the metal in the road? Look, he's over

to the right on the grass, sitting up and pulling off his helmet."

"Hit-and-run?"

"Hard to tell," she said. "Hopefully, the fact that he's sitting up is a good sign."

"Can you get a signal on your phone yet?" Ben asked.

Sara shook her head as she held her cell up, eyes locked on the screen. "No, still only one bar."

Ben pulled the car over, but before he'd pulled on the emergency brake Sara had the door open and was racing toward the victim.

"Get your bag," she called over her shoulder. "My duffel, too."

By the time he grabbed the bags and dropped them on the ground next to her, Sara was kneeling in the grass talking to the victim, who was dressed in a black leather jacket, jeans and boots. The young man's helmet lay next to him, intact except for some scratches and dust.

Ben began a mental assessment of the victim. *Male. Caucasian. Approximately twenty years of age. Five feet six. Fair skin and blond hair.*

Without warning, a wave of nausea slammed into Ben, and a vicious stampede of his own heart rate began. His only defense was to swallow hard and hold on tight.

Ben recognized the symptoms. The onset of a panic attack. *Lord, no,* he silently prayed. Not now. This was only supposed to happen in the hospital.

Fight it. Fight it. He repeated the words like a mantra in his head.

Taking a deep breath, he tossed Sara a package of latex gloves and tore open one for himself. "Collision with a car?" he asked, feigning normalcy.

"No," the young man insisted. "I let the bike down. It's just my leg. I think it got caught between the bike and the ground, then we both slid."

"Eddie says a jackrabbit ran in front of the bike," Sara said. "The accident happened about fifteen minutes ago."

"Eddie?" Ben asked.

"Yes. Eddie, this is Dr. Rogers. Eddie's given us consent to treat." She turned her head to look up at Ben and gasped, her eyes widened. "Ben, what's wrong?"

"Nothing." Ben wiped perspiration from his brow with his forearm. "Any significant medical history?" he asked.

Sara narrowed her eyes, watching Ben as he knelt down on the other side of Eddie. "No medical history to speak of, and no allergies. He denies head trauma," she said.

Ben nodded and looked at Eddie. "We're going to try to move you as little as possible, but we do need to do a quick exam. I'm going to unzip your jacket and listen to your lungs and heart first."

When he finished, Ben took the stethoscope from his ears and gave Sara a nod. "Lungs clear. Heart regular in rhythm and rate."

Sara slipped on her gloves, her eyes never leaving Ben. "Penlight?"

He fished one out of his bag.

"Pupils are equal and reactive," she said.

"Can you squeeze my hands?" Ben asked. Eddie complied.

"Great," Ben said. "Where do you hurt?"

"My left leg hurts like you wouldn't believe."

Ben slipped two fingers under the tongue

of the boot to gently palpate the pedal pulses. "I'd like to leave the boots on if we can. Tell me if you can you wiggle your toes inside them?"

"Yeah," Eddie answered.

Sara nodded to Ben as she pulled a utility knife from her cargo pants. Eddie's jeans were already torn, and a five-centimeter area on his thigh was saturated with blood. Sara quickly sliced through the denim fabric at the ankle.

Ben reached out and tore the denim until the entire leg was exposed. He released a breath at the sight.

Eddie had sustained a ten-inch ragged laceration with abrasions on his thigh in the fall on the rocks and gravel. The entire area was studded with dirt and gravel.

While the area was bleeding, it didn't appear that he'd severed any major blood vessels. The penetration was thankfully not deep into the muscle tissue. His gaze met Sara's, and in an instant they silently agreed on treatment. Rinse the site, cover and apply pressure until they got to the E.R. where it could be properly cleansed and evaluated.

She nodded to Ben as she twisted open two bottles of water. "This is going to be cold."

"Yeah, it is," Eddie said. He jerked as the water splashed against his skin.

"Sorry about that." Sara poured a continuous stream of water over the cut until the bottles were empty.

When she finished, Ben tore open a box of sterile gauze pads and reached forward to hold pressure at the site. "Lower extremity fracture," he observed, assessing the angle of the leg. "Impossible to tell the degree of damage without an X-ray."

"Ice," Sara said. She wasted no time as she raced to the Land Rover.

"Sara's a doctor too, right?" the young man asked.

"She sure is," Ben said. "One of the best."

Sara returned with a T-shirt wrapped around a bag of ice.

"We're going to need a splint to stabilize the leg," Ben said, still observing the site.

Sara handed Ben the ice and glanced around. "I'll get some sticks. I've got hiking boots on, and you don't." She gave him another slow look. "You're sure you're all right?"

"I'm good." And he was. The initial panic symptoms had abated. "I'll stay with Eddie and continue to monitor his vitals."

"Be right back, then," she said.

"Are you from around here?" Ben asked. He shifted positions, continuing to maintain pressure on the thigh wound.

"Paradise. My dad runs the feed store."

Ben used his other hand to recheck Eddie's pulse, counting as the kid kept talking.

"I work there part-time when I'm home on summer breaks from college."

Ben nodded.

Without warning, Eddie's face crumpled. "My mother is going to have a fit."

"Hey, hey, it's okay. I'll vouch for you." Ben gave him an awkward pat on the arm. "This wasn't your fault."

"Tell my mother that."

"So what happened?" Ben asked.

"The rabbit came out of nowhere. I knew I was going down, so I tried to slide out and roll away from the bike. I don't know what happened, but my leg turned wrong when I rolled, and I hit something solid on the side of the road."

Ben looked over at the helmet. "That helmet probably saved your life, and that leather jacket protected you from some serious road rash."

"Be sure to tell my mother that, too. The helmet cost a week's pay."

"I will," Ben agreed.

"Got 'em," Sara said, out of breath as she dropped the bundle on the ground.

Ben turned, his eyes widening as he stared at the pile of sticks. "That's a lot of branches."

"I have plans for the big ones." Sara stood. Selecting two sticks, she began to cut away the knots from the branches, wrapping gauze rolls around the bumps in the wood to provide smooth splints. Kneeling down, she measured them against the outside and inside of Eddie's leg.

Ben pulled back the 4x4s and peered at the wound. The bleeding had slowed enough to secure the site with medical tape while they fashioned the splint.

"There are more gauze rolls in my bag," Ben said.

"We can use that to fill in the voids. Can

you grab that big towel from the duffel and position it around his foot for stabilization?"

Ben checked Eddie's pedal pulses once again before cradling the towel around his boot. "All set."

Sara pulled a long-sleeved T-shirt from the bag and pulled out her knife again. "Let's cut this into strips."

"Got it," Ben said as he began tearing the fabric.

"I'll hold his leg, you slide the strips underneath and shimmy them up his leg. We'll secure the splint above and below the fracture and at the ankle to hold the towel."

Ben began to thread the strips under Eddy's leg. When he finished, he looked up. "So no chance of medical response?" he asked Sara.

"No signal until we get down the mountain. The irony is that by then, we'll be close enough to the Paradise Hospital E.R. to take him ourselves. So we may as well transport."

"Transport." Ben repeated the word. Suddenly the value of the new clinic and thinking outside the box for medical response to meet the needs of the community became very, very real.

"Yes. And soon, the temps at this altitude start to drop much faster than the valley."

"You know, I think I can walk," Eddie said.

"No." Both he and Sara said the word in unison. Ben's eyes met Sara's, and he lowered his voice. "So you're sure you don't have a backboard and a collar in that duffel?"

"Don't I wish. But I do have a plan."

"I never doubted it," Ben said.

She gave a small chuckle. "The sleeping bag."

"What?" Ben asked.

"We turn it inside out and position those two branches I collected, securing them to the zipped bag with duct tape to make a blanket stretcher. Eddie's not too tall. He'll easily fit into the back of your Land Rover with the seats down."

Ben glanced from the victim to his vehicle. She was serious. "You're amazing."

"Wilderness training." She shrugged. "It's really not a big deal."

"Yeah it is," he said. Ben stepped away from Eddie for a moment and turned his back on their victim, his next words for Sara's ears only. "We better move fast. I'm concerned about the possibility of internal injuries. Let's change that gauze on the laceration once more. You can hold the pressure while I drive. Right now he's stable, but if he loses any more blood he may get shocky."

Sara nodded in agreement.

"I'll move seats down in the Land Rover." Ben jogged to the car and tossed the supplies to the front passenger seat floor. Moving fast, he shoved down the passenger seat and the middle three seats as Sara began to tape the branches around the sleeping bag.

"Ready," she called.

"Let's log-roll him onto the stretcher. You take his head, shoulders and chest. I'll handle the lower extremities."

Sara turned to Eddie. "Let us do the work."

Eddie nodded.

"Okay, pull him over," she instructed.

"That's it," Ben said as they carefully moved Eddie. "Now let's shove some of that extra clothing you brought around his head to immobilize him for the ride." Working together, Ben balled the clothing and Sara added duct tape.

"Good," Ben said. "Ready to lift?"

Sara nodded.

"On three. One. Two. Three," he directed.

"Let me get in the vehicle, and we can slide him in," Sara said as she scrambled into the rear of the vehicle.

"Eddie, how are you doing?" Ben asked.

"Oh, I've been better." He gave them a weak smile.

"Yeah, I imagine," Ben returned.

"Okay if I take a nap?"

"No," Sara answered. "We want you awake and talking until we get to Paradise."

"All set?" Ben asked as he prepared to close the back of the vehicle.

"I am," Sara said. She pulled her cell from a pocket. "Eddie, what's your folks' number? I want to get it in my cell before we get to the E.R."

"Do we have to call them?" Panic washed over his face.

"Is there a problem with calling your parents?" She paused and looked at Eddie.

"My mom is going to kill me."

"I'm thinking not. She's going to be pretty happy you're in one piece," Ben commented.

Eddie grimaced. "I really don't think it's a

good idea to call them." He opened his mouth and closed it, struggling for words. "Look, my…my sister died five years ago. I'm all they have, and my mom was totally against me getting this bike. They're going to freak out. I don't want to upset them."

Sensing Eddie's mounting agitation, Ben motioned for Sara to get out, and he climbed in the rear of the Land Rover.

"Eddie, take it easy, man," he soothed. "It's going to be okay." Ben took a deep breath, knowing he had to say the words. This kid needed to know he wasn't alone. "Look, I get it. I lost my sister six months ago."

"Yeah?" Eddie said, his eyes searching Ben's. "I'm real sorry."

"Me, too." Ben paused, maintaining eye contact. He swallowed hard, his mouth dry. "Why don't I go tell your parents in person? Would that help?"

"Yeah, it would. Especially with you being a doctor and all. They'd believe you if you said I was okay."

"Then that's what I'll do." Ben nodded. "So we're good?"

"Yeah. We're good." Eddie smiled. "Thanks. Thanks a lot."

"No problem."

"You know what?" Eddie said.

Ben turned back and raised his brows in question.

Eddie lowered his voice. "You and that cute doctor, Sara—you two make a good team."

"You think?" Ben gave a small chuckle.

Eddie nodded.

Ben jumped out of the SUV. When he turned, his gaze slammed into Sara's. Her eyes were moist, the green irises clouded with compassion.

"Ben, I…" She released a breath. "I didn't realize you'd lost your sister. I'm so sorry."

"Thanks."

Her lips formed a grim line. "I feel so foolish for joking about your stethoscope."

Reaching out, he put his hand on her shoulder and gently squeezed. "Sara. It's okay." He glanced toward the back of the SUV. "We need to get going."

She simply nodded.

Ben slowly exhaled, and as he did the paralyzing pain that had gripped his heart for so long lessened a little bit.

The doors of the E.R. burst open as they approached. Medical personnel were already running toward them with a gurney.

"Dr. Sara Elliott," Sara said to a nurse in blue scrubs, who was carrying a very official clipboard. "We have a twenty-one-year-old male, motorcycle accident. Laceration and abrasions to the right thigh with probable lower extremity fracture. Mental status is stable. No indication of head trauma. Pulse seventy-two, regular. His name is Eddie Connealy. Family notification is being done by Dr. Ben Rogers."

"Great. You've covered everything. Thanks."

"My bike? What about my bike?" Eddie called out as two orderlies transferred him to the gurney.

"I'll take care of it," Ben said from behind her.

"Thanks, man."

"No problem."

"I'm going in with him," Sara said.

Ben nodded. "I'll go talk to his folks, and then I'm going to pick up his motorcycle."

"But how?" Sara asked.

"My buddy Orvis Carter has a truck. I'll take the bike to Eddie's parents' house," Ben said. He got back in the Land Rover. "I'll call you when I'm done. Okay?"

"Okay," she answered, still perplexed at his sudden departure.

"Sara?"

Sara turned and grinned. "Hey, Sam," she greeted Sam Lawson, Paradise's local law enforcement. Tall, dark and lean, Sheriff Sam Lawson was one of the few men in Paradise without a senior discount card. That made him a target for every eligible female in town. Sam handled it well, with a no-trespass sign and tall fences around his personal life. Sara respected that, especially since she knew he still mourned the loss of his wife.

"Nice work," Sam said. He removed his sunglasses and smiled.

"I had help."

"So I heard. Dr. Ben Rogers. He's number one on Bitsy's most-wanted list these days."

"Oh?"

"She claims he's hiding from her."

Sara laughed. "That's just hilarious."

"Yeah. I like the guy already." Sam's grin widened. "You want to tell me what happened with Eddie?"

"He was avoiding an animal in the road. There were no indications that another vehicle was involved, and I don't think he was speeding."

"Okay, good, but I'm going to need you to fill out some paperwork on the accident."

"Oh, Sam, can it wait until tomorrow? I'm exhausted."

"Sure. Bitsy takes lunch at twelve-thirty. Might be a good time to stop by." He winked and gave her a nod as he opened the door to his patrol car.

"Got it," Sara said. She moved swiftly through the E.R. automatic doors, where she found her uncle waiting in the lobby.

"What are you doing here on a Saturday, Uncle Henry?"

Henry Rhoades blinked. His white hair was mussed as usual. "Me? Oh, I was catching up on some paperwork for the clinic. They called me to say you were coming in with an accident victim. Nicely done, dear."

"Thanks, but we were just in the right place at the right time. The victim is Eddie Connealy. His parents run the Feed & Seed downtown. He has a leg fracture and a laceration, and hopefully that's all."

Henry nodded and glanced around. "Where's Ben?"

"He's notifying Eddie's parents and taking care of Eddie's motorcycle."

"So Ben didn't actually go into the hospital?"

"Into the hospital? No." Sara narrowed her eyes. "Why?"

"Just a theory I'm working on."

"Are you going to tell me?"

"Not right now, dear." He smiled. "So you two were out today?"

"Yes. I was showing him the community. Didn't you get my message?"

"Yes. I believe I did." Henry wagged his brows.

"Don't get any ideas, Uncle Henry. You know I didn't come back to Paradise for anything like that."

"If you say so." He wheeled his chair around.

"I mean it, Uncle Henry. We were only out because Ben said you inspired him to get to know Paradise and the needs of the community."

Henry stopped and turned his head. "I like that young man."

Sara laughed. "Yes. I know. Which is why it's going to be very interesting to see what you decide when the clinic opens."

"What makes you think I haven't already decided?"

She blinked and shook her head at her cagey uncle. "I am much too tired to figure out what you mean by that. I think I'll go check on Eddie."

"You look tired, Sara. Go home. I'll have the staff call you and let you know how he's doing."

"Thank you so much, Uncle Henry."

She searched her phone contacts for Ben's number and hit Send.

"Sara?"

"Yes. Ben, did you take care of the bike?"

"I did. I got a hold of Orvis, and one of his sons is picking it up and taking it to the body shop in town. Eddie can claim it there. Oh, and his parents are on the way."

"That was awfully nice of you."

"Least I could do after watching you in action."

She paused. Had she been too assertive, taking over the situation?

"How's Eddie?" Ben asked.

"In X-ray. My uncle will have the hospital call when they know more."

"Nice to know people in high places."

"Sometimes," she agreed.

"So our day was interrupted," Ben said. "What are your plans for dinner?"

"I hadn't thought about it." She glanced at her watch, surprised at the time. "It's getting late."

"Yeah. I'm hungry and I want to eat, but I sure don't want to eat in Paradise and run into the Ladies' Auxiliary."

"They've got a good restaurant in Four Forks up the road."

"Four Forks? That's a town?" Ben asked.

"Yes. Four forks in the road and four stoplights. Get it?"

"I do. But how about we throw some steaks on the grill at my place. It's closer."

Taken off guard, Sara hesitated before answering. "Sure. I'll get my car and meet you at your place."

"Great."

"Do you want me to pick up anything on the way?"

"No. I went grocery shopping on Wednesday night this time, per your instructions. Not a single member of the Ladies' Auxiliary in sight."

She laughed. "Now you're getting the hang of things."

"Yeah. That should worry me."

She could hear the smile in his voice.

"So I'll see you in a half hour or so?" Ben asked.

"Yes," Sara said. She punched the end button and stood for a moment, staring at the screen.

For the past two years, since the defection of her fiancé, she'd avoided men. It was ridiculous, she knew. No one in Boulder knew her father. There was no way Hollis could have manipulated anyone into dating the rancher's daughter.

No, that wasn't it. The bottom line was that she no longer trusted her judgment. How could she have missed all the signs pointing to the fact that the man she was about to marry wasn't in love with her?

Why was she suddenly willing to take a chance again? Yes, that was the question running through her mind. Why now? Why Ben?

How had he moved past her defenses so easily? She respected Ben, and more than that, she was beginning to really like him as a person. But it was the growing attraction between them, which she was unable to deny, that really worried her.

They were competing for the same job, the same chance for a future in Paradise.

Sara pulled her keys from her pocket and sighed. She knew the symptoms and could identify the diagnosis clearly. Someone was going to end up with a serious case of heart-ache. Most likely her. Yet here she was, ignoring the flashing lights and sirens, unable to resist the temptation Ben Rogers presented.

Chapter Eight

Sara drove right past the cabin. She sat in the Jeep for a moment, perplexed. Backing up the car, she stopped and stared.

Yes, it *was* Ben's cabin, but with a brand-new porch, and something had changed with the yard. The tall overgrown bushes guarding the driveway were gone. No wonder she'd missed the turn.

The front door opened, and Ben stepped outside and leaned against the railing. No fair. He'd showered and changed. Now he stood there with his dark hair wet and combed back, looking like an ad for something dangerously masculine.

"What do you think?" he called out.

Sara opened her car door. "Wow, it's beautiful. Who did this?" She pulled a sweatshirt from the front seat and tugged it on over her dusty shirt.

"I'm guessing Orvis, Anna and their son the carpenter. I've only been gone twelve hours, so they must have had help."

"A porch-raising party. Too bad we missed it." Sara moved up the steps, stopping to run her hand over the smooth pine of the handrail. "He's quite the craftsman."

"You said it."

"So do you paint this or stain it?"

"I'm going to have to confer with the porch fairy and get back to you."

"I thought you were into this stuff," she said as she walked back and forth, admiring the new planks.

"I thought so, too, until I came home and saw my porch."

She laughed and leaned over the rail. "Did someone clean up the front yard?"

"Yeah. The lawn boy."

"What? You hired a lawn boy? Isn't that contrary to your do-it-yourself credo?"

"Yeah." He chuckled. "It would be, except that I'm the lawn boy. I did the yard."

She turned toward Ben and laughed. "Nice job."

"Thanks."

"What do you have there?" she asked, nodding toward a foil-covered plate on the porch floor.

Ben turned and frowned. "Now how did I miss that?" He picked up the dish. "Someone must have dropped it off when I was in the shower."

"It's pie," Sara said, unable to hold back her glee. She knew only too well where that pie came from.

Ben peeled back the foil, revealing a deep golden-brown crust. Slices of light brown peaches bathed in a thick caramel juice peeked through the slits in the crust.

"Yum. Homemade peach pie," Sara said.

"Who leaves peach pie on doorsteps?" Ben asked.

"You aren't from around here. This is trademark Bitsy Harmony."

His eyes rounded. "Great. They found me."

"That was inevitable. But once you taste this pie, you'll be forgiving. Trust me. Bitsy is known throughout the county for her pies.

Grown men have been brought to their knees by Bitsy's pies."

"Sara." Ben released a frustrated breath. "It's not the pie I'm concerned about."

"Stop worrying. We'll find a project for Bitsy and her crew."

He glanced around his yard, brow furrowed. "Apparently not fast enough."

Sara raised her head and sniffed the air. Her stomach growled in response. "Now I smell steak."

"Yeah, come on. And hurry—I need to turn them, or we'll end up eating peanut butter and jelly instead of Kansas City strip steaks."

Sara followed Ben through a maze of boxes stacked in the cabin and out the backdoor. As she stepped into the little yard she stopped and did a double-take.

The lawn was a neatly cut green carpet that stretched to the perimeter, which was marked with a border of conifers. Closer to the house, beneath a cluster of tall aspens, a picnic table was set up, complete with a checkerboard tablecloth and dishes.

In the trees above the table, glass canning jars filled with short, squat white candles were suspended with wire. To the right, a hammock hung from a metal stand swayed gently in the late-afternoon breeze.

"Oh, my goodness. This yard is amazing. Did you do this, as well?"

Ben shrugged, then opened the lid of a monster stainless-steel-and-black porcelain gas grill. Smoke billowed out as he flipped the steaks with metal tongs. "I went into Monte Vista after my fiasco in town and picked up yard stuff. And I ordered the grill at the local hardware store."

"Nice grill. Looks like it will do everything but the dishes."

"Pretty much."

"So where did you pick up the dog?" she asked.

"*Dog?* What dog?"

Sara pointed to a chaise lawn chair where a small, dirt-colored mutt with matted fur was stretched out, watching them hopefully.

"That one," she said. "Nice touch, by the way." She waved a hand slowly around the yard. "This looks like it's ready to be photographed for a magazine."

Ben blinked as though he was seeing things. "He's not mine."

"I don't know. He looks awfully comfortable. Are you sure he didn't come with the place?"

"What he looks is dirty."

"Yes. Now that you mention it, he does. Goodness, his fur is all matted and full of briars. And he looks hungry, too. Poor thing."

"Don't get any ideas," Ben warned.

"Oh, come on." She put her hands on her hips and gave him her most indignant stare. "It's just a dog. A little one, too."

"I'm serious, Sara. It's not good to get emotionally attached to a stray dog."

She laughed, because that was pretty much the silliest thing she had ever heard. "Life is all about getting emotionally attached to stray dogs, Ben."

He released a breath. "Okay then—you live on a ranch, you take the little dog back with you."

"I've brought home my share of strays. Plenty, believe me. Right now I'm only staying at the ranch temporarily." Sara narrowed her eyes and looked him up and down. "Have you ever even had a dog?"

"No. I told you, my parents traveled a lot when I was growing up. Missions and all. And, well, my condo has pet restrictions."

Sara smiled as she slowly sat down on the chaise next to the animal, allowing him to sniff her. "Of course it does. So this is perfect."

Ben plopped down into a chair opposite her and narrowed his eyes. "How do you figure?"

"Mutt here needs a home, and you need a roommate." She lifted her shoulders at the simple logic.

"He might already have a home," Ben offered.

"Doubtful." She stroked the pup on his head, and he leaned into her fingers, eyes closed, enjoying the attention and the massage. "No collar, and look at his condition. I'd say someone dropped him off."

"People do that?"

"Up here? Yes, all the time. You'd be surprised. Need to get rid of your dog or your cat, then take them on a one-way trip to the country. After all, animals love the country.

Right? What they don't realize is that most of the time these animals become a tasty lunch for the mountain critters."

Ben's face mirrored horror and disgust. "Okay. Okay. Fine." He ran a hand over his face. "He can stay—for a little while. But that's all I'm committing to."

Sara perked up at his words. That was all she needed. Mutt here was as good as adopted.

"And what makes you think I need a roommate?" Ben asked, suspicion steeling his voice.

"You're all alone out here, Ben."

"I told you. I like alone."

"No one likes alone." Sara said the words softly.

Ben stared at her, looking confused. With a frown, he got up. "I have to get the corn from the house."

"Could you get a bowl of water, too?"

"You need a bowl of water? For what?" he fairly growled.

"For Mutt, of course."

"Mutt? You've named him Mutt?"

Sara smiled serenely.

"Mutt," Ben mumbled under his breath, and shook his head as he went into the house.

Sara continued to stroke the small dog. She leaned down next to his floppy little ear and whispered, "Don't let him scare you. Ben's really a marshmallow on the inside. You're going to be very good for him. He thinks he's a loner, but he's not."

Mutt looked at her with his big brown eyes, as if he understood that they had to be patient with Ben. After all, anything really good was worth waiting for.

Sara smiled in complete agreement.

Ben figured he could sit here all night with Sara. The two of them lounged on his new lawn chairs, relaxing after their steak dinner. Above their heads the candle jars glowed, bathing them in a soft light as the sun began a slow descent in the evening sky.

Sara sighed. "This is really nice."

"It is."

"Thanks for dinner. That was probably the best steak I've had in a long time, too." She cleared her throat. "But don't tell the Cattle King I said that."

"Your secret is safe with me," Ben said. "This was the least I could do after you played tour guide."

Sara nodded. "We'll do it again sometime. There's still a lot more to show you."

"I've already gained quite a bit of knowledge because of today's trip."

"Oh?" she queried.

"Well, I can definitely see how getting up there in the winter could be a problem. But what I haven't figured out is a solution."

"We've talked about snowmobile teams," Sara said.

"Like a volunteer service?"

"Yes. On-call teams. Like the volunteer fire department in Paradise."

"Definitely would be well utilized. Has anyone considered a mobile clinic?" Ben asked.

"A mobile clinic?"

"Like bloodmobiles, in RVs or buses." He shook his head. "Why not utilize a clinic on wheels that would make stops in the community, bringing immunizations, minor medical appointments, vision testing to the community? In the summer, it could visit those RV camping sites to tackle minor first-aid issues."

"That is a seriously awesome idea," Sara said, her eyes wide with excitement.

"I thought so. In fact, your free clinic could operate from the clinic on wheels." He frowned. "That reminds me. Have you heard how Eddie's doing?"

"I'm sorry," Sara said. "I forgot to tell you. The hospital called on my way over. No complications. They're monitoring his neuro status, and he'll probably be discharged on Monday with a nice cast and a dozen sutures."

"Good. I like Eddie. He's a nice kid."

"There are a lot of nice folks in Paradise," Sara commented.

"Yeah. I'm starting to agree."

"Despite your concerns about the Ladies' Auxiliary?"

Ben gave her a short smile. "The jury is still out on them."

They were silent for a moment, both lost in their own thoughts, when she finally spoke.

"Ben?"

"Hmm?" He turned to Sara.

"I'm sorry about your sister." Her brows were knit with concern as she said the words.

"I don't presume to know your grief, and if I said anything that was out of line when we were talking today, I apologize."

"No worries, and ah, thanks." There was nothing more to say. Life had been one continuous condolence for the past six months. Sorry. Sorry. Sorry.

Just for tonight, he wanted to stop being sorry.

"Why did you let me babble on about your stethoscope?"

"You weren't babbling."

"You know what I mean. Why haven't you mentioned this before?" she asked.

"It's only been six months, Sara. I wish I could talk about it…but I can't."

"Fair enough. But when you want to talk, well, just know that I'm here."

He nodded.

She shifted, and Mutt stirred in her lap.

"He's snoring," Ben noted.

"Poor thing is exhausted after that bath I gave him."

"You're going to smell like wet dog," Ben said.

"Oh, I don't care." She shrugged. "I can't smell much worse than I already do."

"You're kind of an unusual woman."

"Me?" She looked at him.

"Yeah, I'm not accustomed to low maintenance."

"And that's kind of sad, isn't it?" Sara looked from the pitiful pup to him and sighed.

"Well, most of the women I know aren't part wilderness scout either," he teased.

Her lips twitched. "I'm glad I could fill that void in your life."

Ben grinned at her response.

Once again a comfortable silence stretched between them. Finally, Sara glanced at her watch. "I've got to get going. Church tomorrow."

Reluctant to end the evening, he listened but didn't answer as she kept chatting.

"It's a nice little church right in downtown Paradise. Small congregation. You should stop by sometime."

"I'll give that some thought," he said.

"Don't think too much, Ben. I'm guessing that's one of your talents."

Ben narrowed his eyes at her challenge. "Does the Ladies' Auxiliary gang attend there?"

"They aren't a gang. And yes, they do. There's a spot set aside for their Harleys."

He chuckled.

Mutt whined as Sara slowly stood and set him on the ground. "Mutt is getting spoiled already."

"So that's really his name?"

Sara nodded. "Yes. I like it." She reached for the stack of dishes on the picnic table.

Ben's hand collided with hers, and they both froze. "Leave them," he said.

"I'm only going to bring them in the house. We're going that way, anyhow."

He shook his head, knowing there was no point arguing. Sara liked to get the last word. Family trait, he figured. Ben held the door open for her, and the little dog trailed into the house, as well.

"Just set them in the sink."

Sara looked around the cabin like she had the first time she'd stopped by, as though there was some secret to unearth about him in the place.

"Interesting decorating choices."

"The boxes or the boxes?"

"Both." She turned around. "Does that fancy coffee machine really make good coffee?"

"It sure does."

"It certainly is pretty, I'll give you that." She bent over and examined the sleek stainless steel, touching the knobs.

"I could make you an espresso," he offered.

Her eyes lit up before she shook her head. "I better not. If I drink it now, I won't have a chance of sleeping. Next time."

"Sounds good," Ben murmured. Yeah, he definitely liked the sound of next time.

Mutt began investigating the cabin, alternately trotting around, his nails clicking on the hardwood floor, and stopping to sniff the old furniture.

"Am I going to have to take this dog outside to do his business?"

"Don't worry," Sara said. "Mutt will train you in the basics. He'll tell you exactly what he needs."

"That's the part I'm worried about."

She shook her head, letting him know in no uncertain terms that Mutt was staying with him.

"What about work?" he asked.

"What about work?" she returned as she pulled her car keys from a pocket.

"I can't leave him home in the cabin all day by himself."

"Bring him to the clinic."

"You've got to be kidding," Ben said.

"My uncle loves dogs. Besides, until the end of August we won't have any employees on site."

"Except the office manager," Ben returned.

"The interview is on Monday. We'll make sure she likes dogs, too," Sara said.

He slowly shook his head. "That seems pretty presumptuous criteria, considering I might not even be here in September."

"You need to have a more positive outlook, Dr. Rogers."

"We both want the job, Sara. I'm pretty *positive* about that."

"Well, I'm turning the situation over to God. As you recommended."

"I did?" he said.

She looked at him. "Yes. You said to pray. You were right. Pray and let go. That leaves a lot of room for the Lord to work. I believe He can do the impossible."

"And I believe I have a big mouth," Ben said.

Sara laughed, and the keys in her hand fell to the ground. They both reached for them at the same time. Once again, their hands met. This time Ben didn't freeze.

Instead he picked up the keys. They straightened in slow motion, eyes locked on each other. With deliberation, Ben reached out to carefully tuck a wayward lock of dark hair behind Sara's ear. His hand lingered.

She inhaled, holding her breath as he gently touched the scar, his fingers moving lightly over the thin silver line.

"I'm so sorry," Ben said.

"Don't be," she whispered. "It's part of who I am."

He moved to weave his fingers in her hair until he gently cupped the back of her head. Leaning in, he inhaled, his eyes fixed on her mouth until her eyelids fluttered closed.

Sara sighed as his lips touched her warm mouth. For moments they stood, lost in a sweet mix of longing and simplicity.

Ben moved away, dropping his hand and clearing his throat. "I'm sorry."

Sara slowly shook her head. "Ben, you're sorry much too much."

He released a pained breath. "Am I? Funny, I was thinking the same thing earlier."

"Don't be sorry," she said.

"We have to work together. I don't want to make you uncomfortable, Sara."

"I'm not uncomfortable." She shrugged. "It was just a kiss. Besides, I have no intention of starting anything I can't finish. My focus is on my career and my father right now. That's plenty."

Despite her words, he couldn't help but notice the flush of pink on her cheeks. Oh, yeah, the kiss had touched her deeply. As much as it had him.

"Right," he said.

"I'd better get going." She opened the front door and stepped out into the night.

Ben followed her out to the porch.

At the Jeep, she turned and looked at him. "The offer is still good for church. The Lord has a seat reserved for you."

"Oh, I'm sure He does."

Sara's smile seemed almost sad, and Ben felt the tug of emotion as she got into the car.

Mutt trotted outside, and together they watched her drive off. Ben shook his head as he glanced down at the little dog. A dog and a woman in his life.

Lord, things are starting to get complicated.

He didn't want more opportunities to let anyone down. But it seemed the more he ran from involvement, the more involvement life was dishing up.

Chapter Nine

On Monday, Ben pushed open the door to the chapel garden, surprised to find the hospital medical director there. "Dr. Rhoades?"

Henry Rhoades spun around in his wheelchair. "Ben, good morning. You know, I think it's about time you got used to calling me Henry."

"Sir?"

"Henry. That's my name."

"Yes, sir. I mean, Henry."

"What's that you have there?"

Ben glanced down at Mutt, who had followed him to the garden.

"It's a dog," Ben said.

"Yes, I can see that."

Mutt trotted over to Henry Rhoades and

rubbed his head against his leg, begging for attention. Henry smiled and obliged, rubbing the little dog's head.

"He stays in my office."

"I wasn't worried. Merely curious."

"Sara assigned him to me."

When Henry burst out with a belly laugh, Ben could only respond with a weak smile.

"That sounds like Sara. What's his name?"

"Mutt."

"Here, Mutt." The little dog jumped into Henry's lap. "Smart dog." Henry rubbed Mutt's ears and smiled. "Mutt is certainly welcome in the clinic, although I recommend doggie day care when the accreditation inspection process begins."

"Yes, sir."

"Anything I can do for you, Ben?"

"I was wondering if I could help *you?* I didn't expect to see you in here today."

"I have to admit, the closer we get to September, the more excited I am about the clinic opening. I'm doing my best not to micromanage, but I find myself down here at least once a day to see how things are coming along.

Since I'm here, I can't miss an opportunity to visit my favorite spot."

Ben glanced around at the barren soil. "But the gardens aren't completed."

"In here it is." Henry tapped his forehead. "So, how *are* things coming along?"

"Very well. We hired the office manager this morning. She starts next week, and she'll take over interviewing and hiring the rest of the office staff. Housekeeping has been hired, as well. We have two physician's assistants on board, one with a background in women's health and the other in pediatrics. We've also started on the paperwork for the certification process."

"Splendid. What about the staff physicians?"

"We're interviewing again this week. This time we might get lucky."

"Let's hope so."

"Sir—I mean, Henry—since you're here, I have something to run by you."

"Yes?"

Ben nodded toward the unfinished gardens. "What do you think about the possibility of turning this area into a memorial garden for your sister? Sara's mother."

The older man's eyes rounded with interest. "Tell me what you're thinking."

"You mentioned a gazebo and benches. What about wildflowers from the valley planted in the flower beds? I understand those were her favorite."

Henry smiled. "I think that's a wonderful idea. I'm sorry I didn't think of it myself."

"You do?"

"Oh, yes. Have you mentioned the idea to Sara?"

"No. I thought maybe we could surprise Sara. No one would notice work out here, especially if it was on the weekends. You and I are the only ones who even come out here."

Henry looked him up and down. "You're very intuitive, aren't you?"

"Not that I know of."

"Trust me. You are. Perhaps because you've had a recent loss."

Ben took a deep breath.

"We'd have to get Hollis's permission to name it after Amanda," Henry continued.

"And once again, the unfortunate fact is that there is no funding for the gardens."

"Would Mr. Elliott consider funding the garden?"

"The question is, are you willing to talk to Hollis?"

"Absolutely."

"You don't know Hollis."

"I'm willing to take a chance."

"Well then, I'll set up a meeting for you. On his territory would be best. He gets cranky and unreasonable when he's near the hospital. Hollis blames the medical profession as a whole for his wife's death. In fact, I suggest you avoid any discussion of medicine at all. Stay on neutral ground, and there is the outside chance he just might agree to your ideas."

"Yes, sir."

Henry glanced at his watch. "I have an appointment. Can you push that button for me?"

Ben scooped Mutt off his lap and pushed the handicap access button. They both moved through the door and into the hallway.

"By the way, you and Sara did an amazing job assisting Eddie after his accident. I've heard nothing but glowing reports from the community. That's the kind of PR we need around here."

"I can't take much credit. It was mostly Sara. She doesn't miss a beat."

"On the contrary, it was teamwork. Exactly what both you and Sara are doing here at the clinic."

They turned as Sara came down the hall juggling papers and folders. She did a double take and stopped in front of them.

"Did I miss something?" She looked from her uncle to Ben.

When her glance landed on him, Ben sensed the awkwardness between them. Since their kiss on Saturday, they'd both tried hard to maintain a professional distance. Yet once or twice, Ben found his gaze lingering on her face, remembering the sweet, stolen kiss of last weekend. When Sara had looked up and blushed, he knew she remembered, too.

"Oh, my gosh, did we have a meeting scheduled?" she asked.

"Oh, no, my dear. We were simply chatting."

"About me? I heard my name."

"We were discussing Eddie, actually," Henry said. "And Mutt."

"How's he doing? Eddie, I mean. Have you heard anything?" Sara asked.

"I saw him in town. He's doing well," Henry said.

"I'm so glad." She glanced at Ben as she knelt down to scratch Mutt behind the ears. "And your new companion here is doing well, also?"

"Mutt is taking over my entire life just fine, thanks."

Sara laughed.

"I have to be going," Henry Rhoades said. "Anything you need from me before I head back to the hospital for another boring meeting?"

Ben looked at Sara. "No, sir. I think we have everything under control."

"I'm confident you do," he said. "You two make quite a team."

She gave Ben a cautious glance before smiling at her uncle. "Thank you, Uncle Henry."

A team, Ben mused. Ironic that the team that had impressed the community would no longer be a team in a mere six weeks. His gaze followed Henry's wheelchair down the hall.

Maybe he'd been looking at the situation all wrong. There had to be a compromise somewhere. He just had to dig deeper and find it.

Ben slowly drove his Land Rover through the impressive Elliott Ranch gates. To his left, miles and miles of land stretched before him. Grazing cattle dotted the distant fields, and ahead stood the huge, pillared two-story home.

This was what Sara Elliott called home? Not a modest ranch house, more like a small country mansion—and exactly what he imagined the home of the Cattle King of Paradise Valley to be.

He parked his car, strode up the expansive front steps and rang the bell. A small Hispanic woman answered the door.

"You must be Dr. Rogers—please come in. I'm Malla. Mr. Hollis is in his study. Follow me."

"Yes, ma'am."

The home was right out of a decorating magazine. Ben shook his head. Sara chided him about his expensive toys, yet the Elliott household rivaled anything in his Denver condo. The spacious open areas they walked through were elegantly furnished with southwestern décor. From the high ceilings accented with oak beams to the glossy polished wooden floors covered with rich handwoven rugs, the house spoke of old money and good taste.

He followed Malla to a room at the back of the house. Wide double oak doors opened to a large office. Floor-to-ceiling bookshelves added warmth to the space, and a picture window provided an exceptional view of the land for the master of all he surveyed. Ben stepped in and nodded to the imposing man behind the massive desk as he admired the several Frederic Remington bronzes in the room.

"Sir, I'm Dr. Ben Rogers. Thank you for meeting with me."

Hollis Elliott stood and came around the desk to shake his hand. Sara's father was a tall man, almost as tall as Ben. His shock of white hair was a stark contrast to his black Western shirt and black jeans.

"You're the man competing with Sara for the clinic director position."

Ben paused, contemplating his response. He nodded thoughtfully. "I do have the honor of working with your daughter at the clinic."

"Sara should be director of the clinic, you know. It's what her mother would have wanted."

"Yes, sir, I understand. Sara is a fine physician."

"Where are you from, Dr. Rogers?"

"I'm a Colorado native."

"That's one point in your favor." Hollis narrowed his eyes in a slow assessment when Ben didn't respond to the bated comment. "Have a seat," he finally said.

"Thank you, sir."

"What can I do for you?" Hollis asked.

"Sir, I'd like your permission to name the clinic garden after your wife."

"After Amanda?"

"Yes. The Amanda Rhoades-Elliott Memorial Gardens."

"This was your idea?"

"Yes, sir. It was."

"What do you get out of it?"

Ben nearly jerked back at the words. Once again, he responded after thorough deliberation. Hollis Elliott was doing his best to intimidate.

Ben cleared his throat. "Sir, I greatly respect your wife's career. Her contributions to rural medicine in Colorado are well known throughout the medical profession. I'd like to honor that and her dedication to the Paradise community."

Hollis Elliott once again paused to assess Ben with hard, unflinching eyes. "That's all you want?"

In that moment Ben decided not to mention the much-needed funding. No, it would be a huge error in judgment to allow Hollis Elliott any more leverage over the clinic. Ben would find his own funding. One way or another. The clinic gardens weren't going to be another battleground for control, or stress for Sara if he could prevent it.

"Yes, sir."

The older man took a deep breath. "You have my permission."

"Thank you, sir." Ben stood and reached out across the desk to shake his hand. "Oh, and it's a surprise until the grand opening of the clinic. So if you could not mention anything to Sara, I'd appreciate it."

Hollis gave Ben a short nod of assent. "Fine."

"Thank you, again." Ben turned to leave.

"We're having an open house here at the ranch two weeks from Saturday. Family and friends. We do it every year. Big barbecue. I'd like you to come."

Ben blinked and turned back, taken off guard by the invitation. "Thank you. What time?"

"Things get started around noon. Wear jeans and boots."

Ben nodded.

"You do have boots?"

"Yes, sir. I do."

"Good. Malla will see you out."

The petite housekeeper was at his side as he left the study. She cocked her head and openly assessed him with a knowing smile.

"You like Miss Sara, don't you?"

Ben jerked back at the words. He turned to look at the woman, but her thoughtful gaze never wavered. And he thought Hollis Elliott was formidable

"Sara needs a Godly man. A man who can stand up to her father."

Ben searched for an appropriate response. "Ma'am?"

Malla opened the front door, and followed him to the porch. "I believe the Lord puts people in our paths for a reason. Don't you, Dr. Rogers?"

Immediately Ben had a mental image of Bitsy Harmony and the Ladies' Auxiliary. Confused, he shook his head. "I guess I never thought about it much."

"Maybe you should," Malla said.

"Yes, ma'am." He nodded and slowly walked down the steps toward his car.

By the time he reached the Land Rover, Sara's Jeep had pulled up the long gravel drive.

Stunned surprise registered on her face as she got out of her car. "Ben, what are you doing here?"

"I had an appointment with your father."

"My—my father?" She paled as she glanced from him to the house, where Malla stood on the porch watching them. Flustered, Sara grabbed her briefcase and purse and slammed the car door. "What could you and my father possibly have to talk about?"

"No big deal. It was about the clinic's grand opening."

As she opened her mouth to speak, Ben gently interrupted. "I have to run, Sara."

And he did. Somewhere in the middle of his talk with Malla, an idea had taken hold in his head and his heart. He nearly shouted at the audacity of the plan. Now he was absolutely certain that the gardens would be completed.

It was almost as if this was the reason God had sent him to Paradise. Wasn't that crazy?

Ben Rogers knew her father? It was her worst nightmare happening all over again. A frisson of panic wrapped itself around her throat until she could barely breathe.

Since last Saturday, she had been doing her best to forget that kiss at Ben's house, struggling to maintain her direction on the path she had determined was her future, and struggling not to lose her heart to Ben Rogers.

Now this?

Lord, tell me this isn't a repeat of two years ago. Tell me I'm just imagining things.

Heart heavy, she walked up the steps where Malla waited at the door.

"I just met your Dr. Ben. He's so very polite and well mannered." A glint of amusement flickered in her eyes. "And handsome, too."

"Malla, he isn't my Dr. Ben."

"Well, then, I have a niece I'd like to introduce to him."

"Emily? The nurse who works at Paradise Hospital?"

Malla nodded. "Unless you don't want me to?"

Their eyes met. Malla was teasing her, trying to evaluate the situation with Ben. Oh, yes, the little housekeeper had been working for Hollis for much too long.

Sara pulled open the door. "Do you have any of that lemonade-and-tea mix left?"

Malla laughed. "Yes. But don't think I don't know what you are up to."

"What?" Sara asked as she dropped her briefcase on the hall chair.

"Avoiding my question."

"I'm not." She picked up the mail and began to sort through the envelopes.

"*Sí, querida,* you are. I think that for the first time, you have met someone who is equal to you. A match."

Sara glanced at Malla and frowned.

A musing smile touched the older woman's lips. "Don't you worry, your Ben, he can handle your father."

"You heard them talking?" Sara dropped the mail and lowered her voice. "Do you know why Ben was here?"

"I don't know." Malla shrugged. "But trust me. I have a feeling about this one."

"Too bad you didn't have a feeling about you-know-who." She refused to even say his name.

"The good Lord doesn't like us to talk badly about people, even if they are no-good, worthless fiancés trying to steal your money and your heart."

Sara sighed. "I seem to be a poor judge of character when it comes to men."

"Don't worry about Ben," Malla said. "He won't break your heart."

Sara shook her head at Malla's words.

Could she be right? Was Ben the one man who could stand up to the formidable Hollis Elliott?

Did she dare let her guard down enough to find out?

"Come, I'll fix you something to eat. You look tired." Malla clucked gently. "It's been a long day, no?"

"Yes. A very long day. I drove to Boulder." Sara reached for her briefcase and pulled out a small bag. "And I stopped at the Boulder Tea House for that tea you love."

"Thank you." Delight lit the housekeeper's eyes as she took the bag. "Now tell me why you were in Boulder."

"I'm being courted by the clinic."

"Oh?"

"They don't want me to resign, and I've been offered some very enticing options."

"But you're going to stay in Paradise." Malla's words were firm.

"Am I?" She shook her head. "I just wish I knew what was going to happen in September. How can I resign from Boulder when my position here is so uncertain?"

Malla took her hand. "You're confused, and confusion is not of the Lord."

Sara released a breath. "I know you're right, but I still don't know what to do about it."

"Where do you feel peace?"

She considered Malla's words for a moment before she answered. "At the Paradise clinic."

"Working with Dr. Ben."

"Yes. Working with Ben." She was unable to hold back the slow smile that parted her lips.

"Then you have your answer, no?"

"But what about September?"

"One day at a time, Sara. Let the Lord take care of tomorrow."

Sara shook her head. The very words she had said to Ben drifted back to her now.

Trust in the Lord with all your heart and lean not unto your own understanding. In all your ways acknowledge Him, and He will direct your paths.

Chapter Ten

"Ladies, we are ready to vote." Bitsy Harmony stood ramrod-straight as she eyed the rows of women like a drill sergeant. A drill sergeant wearing plaid capris with a crisp pink blouse and a white bun anchored on the top of her head. Nonetheless, as far as these troops were concerned, Bitsy was their leader.

Ben glanced around and gave a slight shake of his head. He needed a sanity check because he couldn't believe that he'd purposely walked into a Wednesday-night meeting of the Paradise Ladies' Auxiliary. So far it looked like he was going to live to tell about it, too.

There was a hush in the room as Bitsy tapped her gavel on the podium that had been set up in her living room, and everyone, including Ben, waited for her to continue. Bitsy cleared her throat, and the entire room tensed. "All those in favor of the motion to assist Dr. Rogers with the Covert Clinic Chapel Garden Project, please rise."

There were over three dozen women seated on folding chairs that filled not only the chintz and lace-covered living room, but spilled over into the small dining room. Nearly in unison, every single woman rose.

"The motion passes unanimously."

Ben released the breath he'd been holding, and he couldn't help but grin as a titter of laughter spread like a wave through the members. The women smiled, and several clapped their hands in obvious delight. Even Bitsy's normally austere features had transformed into a joyful countenance at the results of the vote.

"Settle down," Bitsy said. "Remember, this is an undercover operation. That means we don't share information with family, friends or the mail carrier. I have passed out Dr. Rogers's detailed instructions, along with a map of the garden and facility. Anna and Flora are team leaders. Work will commence on

Saturday at 0800, and our deadline is September fourteenth."

"Thank you, ladies," Ben said.

"Dr. Rogers, we're honored to be a part of the project," Bitsy said, once again tapping the gavel. "Is there any more business?" She glanced around. Everyone was silent. "I declare the meeting adjourned and pie served."

Ben stood and pulled his keys from his pockets as Anna Carter approached. "We haven't had this much fun at an auxiliary meeting in years, Dr. Rogers. And we have you to thank for it."

"She's right," Flora Downey added. "The last time was when we planned a surprise wedding for the mayor. Of course, eventually we had to tell him he was getting married."

Ben's eyes rounded, but he knew better than to ask.

"Dr. Rogers, do you mind if I ask how you're funding the project?" Anna said.

Ben swallowed and searched for an appropriately vague response. "Money has been allocated."

"Allocated sounds bureaucratic," Flora returned.

"Won't you join us for pie?" Bitsy asked.

"I'd like that," Ben said, grateful for the interruption. "That peach pie you dropped off at the cabin was the best pie I've ever had."

"Of course it was." Bitsy glowed under his praise. "I've got another all packed up and ready to go."

"Oh, and Dr. Rogers, I brought that special hybrid tomato plant from Orvis for you," Anna informed him. "He said to plant it in a sunny location."

Suddenly he had two dozen mothers. Ben glanced around at the women who filled the tiny cottage. A dull ache filled his heart. He was a grown man, yet today he felt the distance he'd created between himself and his own mother more than ever. He missed her.

He hadn't returned her calls, and he knew he was hurting her. Every day the bridge grew wider, fueled by his fear that he wouldn't be able to hold it together long enough for a conversation.

His sister's death was the obstruction he couldn't circumvent. He just couldn't talk about Carolyn. Even to his folks. Avoidance was the only way he knew to save himself.

"Doctor? Are you all right?" Flora Downey

gently inquired as she touched his sleeve. "Do you need anything?"

He managed a faint smile for Flora as he composed himself. "I'm good."

When Ben finally left Bitsy's house, it was with a peach pie, a raspberry cobbler and a tomato plant in his arms. He shook his head. Sara was right, yet again. The Ladies' Auxiliary, while a force to be reckoned with, was made up of good people.

Three weeks ago he would have never guessed he'd make friends with the same women who'd been stalking him. He nearly laughed aloud at Sara's humorous reference to the Ladies' Auxiliary motorcycle gang, for a moment seeing Bitsy with a helmet atop her tightly wound bun.

These were women who had just voted to give up their Saturdays to support Sara Elliott and the garden project. And they were doing it just because that was what friends and neighbors did.

What a concept. Paradise was teaching him something new every day.

"How did you say you know my father?" Sara asked. It was the third time this week she'd tried to extract information from him. She was trying for subtle and failing miserably.

Ben's lips twitched. He pushed in the bottom drawer of the red cart and stood. "This code cart is ready to go. But I can't find the portable defibrillator."

"It's on order."

"The EKG machine?"

"It came yesterday. I haven't unpacked it yet, and you didn't answer my question, Ben."

"I met your father for the first time the other day at your house—well, *house* seems like an inappropriate term for your homestead. Elliott Ranch looks like a retreat for former presidents. And by the way, why didn't *you* mention that your father has a collection of original Western sculptures in his office?"

"My father has more collections than I care to count. Cars in the garage, artwork and sculptures in the office, baseball card memorabilia in the media room."

"And you harassed me about my espresso machine," he said.

"That's because it grieves me when people waste money on *things*." She checked over the supplies on her list and closed the cupboard door.

"It's his money," Ben pointed out.

"Yes, but it's not what my mother would have wanted," Sara countered.

Ben shoved the crash cart back against the wall. "What would she have wanted?" he asked.

"This." Sara took a deep breath and waved her arm around the exam room they stood in. "Writing a check for new medical equipment would have made her very happy."

"But does it make you happy, Sara?"

"Yes. It does." She paused thoughtfully. "So much so that I turned down the position in Boulder and submitted my resignation."

"Whoa. When did this happen?"

"Monday."

"Monday, and you didn't mention it?" He raised his brows.

"I sort of forgot."

"Forgot? Who forgets they resigned their job?" Ben asked. "I'd bet there's some deeper meaning in that."

"The only deeper meeting was a chat with Malla."

Ben smiled. "I've been on the receiving end of a Malla chat."

"Oh?" She raised her brows.

"That woman is scary insightful."

"Yes. That's Malla."

"So, you've committed to Paradise. Should I be worried?" Ben asked.

"Not any more than you were when we met."

"It's been almost a month. If you had told me six months ago that I'd be in a town the size of Walmart, with a dog no less, preparing to reinvent my medical career and competing with a smart and beautiful doctor for the same position, I'd have thought you were hallucinating."

"I'm beautiful?" She cocked her head, eyes wide in question. "Really?"

"This is news to you?" Ben's gaze skimmed over her features, from her dark lashes that framed her green eyes to her soft, smooth mouth. He found it hard to believe she wasn't aware of her attractiveness, because he sure was. Since their kiss, he'd worked hard not to be aware.

"Let's just say that in the past, my father's money has been more attractive than his daughter when it came to men in my life."

"You've been associating with the wrong men," he said flatly.

"That's obvious." She narrowed her eyes and looked at Ben. "So you're okay with the fact that one of us is going to be director in a few weeks? And the other one is, well…not?"

"I'm not particularly concerned. I think I've been drinking the Paradise Kool-Aid. Or maybe it's the cinnamon rolls from the café. I want the job, Sara. Oh, I definitely want the job, but since I've come to Paradise, I've started to realize that there's a bigger plan for my life."

"A bigger plan? Hmm." She nibbled on her lip for a moment, thinking. "Well, I'm glad you have so much certainty. That makes one of us."

"You're the one who quoted Proverbs," he said.

"The author of Proverbs never met my father."

Ben chuckled. "What's going on with Hollis?"

"I'm not sure, but he doesn't look well. Something is off, I can sense that much. He's avoiding me, too. I can't even get him to sit still so I can listen to his heart or take his blood pressure."

"So what are you going to do?"

"The question is, what can I do? I have an appointment with his cardiologist in Denver. Fortunately my father doesn't remember he signed a HIPAA release form when he had his heart attack."

"Did it ever occur to you that manipulating his health might be his backup plan to keep you in Paradise?"

"I hope you're wrong," she said.

The new office manager, Sue Meredith, popped her head into the clinic exam room. "Excuse me, doctors, but there's an Orvis Carter in the lobby to see Dr. Rogers."

"Thanks, Sue," Ben said.

Sara glanced at the wall clock. "It's nearly five. Were you expecting Orvis?"

"No, but I owe him one. Probably more than one after that porch."

She nodded. "Well, I've got to get going. I have to drive into Monte Vista for my father, but I'll be back tomorrow. We're behind in our accreditation paperwork, and I'd like to get caught up as soon as I can."

Tomorrow was Saturday. The Ladies' Auxiliary would be here to begin planting. He followed Sara as she started down the hall.

"You're coming in tomorrow?"

"Uh-huh," she said.

"You can't come in tomorrow," he said.

Sara turned and looked at him. "Why not?"

"You just said you suspect your father's condition is worsening. Don't you think you should be at home? You spend too much time at the clinic as it is."

She sighed. "I guess you're right. Okay. Fine. I'll work from home."

"Good plan." He nodded, relieved.

Ben left her at her office and headed to the lobby, where Orvis Carter stood next to the counter with a young boy.

"Orvis, what can I do for you?" Ben shook Orvis's hand.

"Doc, this is my grandson, Elijah. We call him Eli."

"Hi, Eli."

Eli grinned, displaying a gap where his front teeth were missing. Ben pegged the young boy at about five or six years old.

"I hate to bother you, but I wondered if you could have a look at his leg."

"Sure. Have a seat, Eli. Do you want to tell me what happened?" Ben asked.

"Gramps says I got bit by a spider," Eli said with a lisp. He sat down in a chair and rolled down his socks, which sported a layer of dirt. Immediately, Ben spotted an expanding area of inflammation.

"When did this happen?" Ben asked.

"I think I felt a bite a few days ago," Eli said.

Ben nodded. "Can you take off that sneaker for me?"

Close to the ankle bone, the skin was not only red and swollen, but there was also a purplish blister in the center of the inflammation.

Ben frowned. "We need to get him treated as soon as possible."

"What is it, Doc?"

"If it is a spider, then a brown recluse is my guess. But I'm not the expert."

Orvis nodded to Ben, and the men moved out of earshot of the boy.

"It's not fatal, is it?" Orvis asked, concern knitting his brows.

"It's serious, but perfectly treatable. I don't suppose you saved the spider?"

"No. Never actually saw it. That boy plays in the dirt so much, we just figured that old spider was still in his shoe."

"That's okay. Either way, Eli needs to get to the emergency room since it's after hours. Or you can drive him into Monte Vista to an urgent care facility."

"We need an urgent care facility here in Paradise."

"I agree, and we're working on that," Ben said.

"What will they do for Eli at the hospital?" Orvis asked.

"There are several different protocols for spider bites, depending on the severity and the age of the victim. Right now we'll elevate Eli's leg, ice the bite and get him to someone with more experience in this area than me."

Orvis nodded. "Then I 'spose we'll go to the emergency room. You'll go with us, won't you?"

Ben inhaled. "I don't have privileges at the

Paradise E.R., but I'll get you all signed in. Will that work?"

"Thank you, Doc."

Minutes later, Ben stood outside the emergency room doors, psyching himself up and praying he could handle the E.R. He wiped a line of sweat from his brow and leaned over to take a deep, calming breath.

"Ben?"

Ben whirled around, surprised when his gaze met Henry Rhoades's.

"Dr. Rhoades."

"Everything all right? You don't look well."

Ben straightened. "I'm, ah, fine sir. It's Orvis Carter. His grandson was bitten by a spider. I need to meet them inside."

Henry positioned his chair away from the doorway to talk to Ben. "Why don't I take care of them for you?"

"I'd hate to inconvenience you, sir."

"Not at all. I'll give Orvis and his grandson the VIP treatment. After all, they're friends of yours."

"Not only friends, but Orvis's son is building the gazebo for the chapel garden."

"Then I insist."

"Thank you, sir." Ben tried not to look as relieved as he felt.

"No problem. Why don't you go home and get an early start on the weekend? You and Sara have put in some long hours this week."

"I might just do that. Thanks."

"Good. Oh, and Ben?"

Ben turned.

"I'd like to chat with you."

"Sure. Any time."

"Schedule an appointment with my secretary for next week."

"Sara, as well?"

"No, I think the two of us is plenty for this discussion. Don't you?"

Ben had no chance to respond to the question before the E.R. doors swung open and Henry wheeled himself inside, leaving Ben to wonder what exactly Dr. Rhoades wanted to discuss with him.

Something told Ben that this was going to be one of those uncomfortable heart-to-hearts that he had avoided most of his life. He shoved his hands in his pocket and walked slowly back to the clinic to pick up Mutt.

The thought of the little dog who would

greet him with exuberant abandon and un-
conditional love, running in circles and lick-
ing Ben's face, made him smile.

While he wasn't ready to admit it out loud
and let Sara throw another "told you so" in his
direction, Ben knew that the little nondescript
dog was part of all the good things that had
happened to him since moving to Paradise.

As a roommate, he was perfect. Mutt never
insisted that Ben share his feelings or questioned what was eating him up inside. And
when Ben sat in the dark, Mutt just curled
up next to him and pretended he was thinking, too.

Ben's pace quickened. He'd been looking
forward to Friday night. The two of them
could enjoy a grilled burger in the backyard
and hang out on the hammock for a while.
The only improvement on that scenario was
if Sara could have joined them. He headed to
the parking lot, whistling under his breath.

In the back of his head a niggling question
surfaced. Why did Dr. Rhoades want to meet
with him? Ben quickly dismissed the thought.

Yeah, he'd worry about the meeting with
Dr. Rhoades later. Much later.

Chapter Eleven

The Pearly Gates were unmanned. Ben glanced up and down the long hallway. This was very unusual.

"Ben?"

Ben whirled around. For a man in a wheelchair, Henry Rhoades sure knew how to sneak up on a guy undetected. Ben considered putting bells on the man's wheelchair.

"What are you doing?" Dr. Rhoades asked.

"Looking for the woman who guards your office."

"Gabriella took a personal day. Apparently she has other things to do besides guard my office and read my mind, along with all the other omniscient duties I require. Imagine that." Henry laughed as he rolled his chair toward his office. "So, Ben, come in. Close the door and have a seat."

"Yes, sir."

"There's coffee over on the sidebar," Dr. Rhoades said as he tidied the papers on his desk.

"No, thank you. I've had my limit this morning."

"Then let's get right to it." He pinned Ben with his gaze. "How are things coming along?"

Ben frowned, confused. "Nothing's changed since I saw you Friday, although I did get a call from Orvis Carter, thanking me for sending the hospital medical director in to take care of his grandson."

"A good man," Henry said. "But let me rephrase my question. How are *you* coming along?"

"Sir?"

"I want you to know that this conversation is strictly off the record."

His mouth suddenly dry, Ben tried to swallow.

Henry continued. "Are you on any medications? Antianxiety? Antidepressant? Sedative?"

This time Ben shot up straight in his chair. *Dr. Rhoades thought he had a drug problem?*

"I'll take that as a no."

"No, sir. I mean, yes, sir."

Henry held up a palm and nodded his understanding. "Have you considered the possibility that a medication regime might be helpful?"

"Excuse me?" He coughed, nearly choking on the words.

"Along with counseling, perhaps a therapist or your pastor."

Again, Ben was stunned silent.

For moments, Henry's green eyes silently and gently probed. "Ben, I'm asking you how you're coping with your sister's death."

For a long moment Ben was unable to move. He was completely unprepared for this conversation. Gripping the arms of the wing chair, he cleared his throat while frantically searching for an appropriate response.

"Sir, I've come a long way, and Paradise has been instrumental in that healing. I believe the Lord sent me here for that reason."

"And yet, you're still having panic attacks."

Ben's head jerked back. "How did you…? Has anyone else…?"

"I doubt if anyone else has put it together. But the truth is. I recognized the symptoms only too well—palpitations, shaking, perspiration, shortness of breath—because I went through much the same thing." He adjusted his glasses. "It took me a year before I stopped breaking out in a cold sweat every time I had to get into an automobile."

Ben's lips formed a thin line as Henry continued.

"I thought perhaps if we talked, I might be able to be a resource for you. Not many people truly understand what you're going through."

"No. That's for sure," Ben agreed.

"How's your relationship with your family?"

"Sir, I, ah, I really don't want to talk about my family."

"That bad?" The older man gave a sympathetic nod. "And what about Sara?"

"Sara?" Ben asked, trying to keep up with the conversation as his emotions ping-ponged back and forth.

"Ben, I'm a paraplegic, but I'm not blind. You and Sara are becoming close."

"I'd like to keep my relationship with Sara strictly professional."

"Have you told your heart that?"

Ben froze as the words reached their target. He rubbed his clammy hands against his pants and stared out the large window. He'd give anything to be somewhere in those mountains right about now, instead of trying to deny to himself the truths Henry was laying out.

"Sir," he finally said. "To tell you the truth, I really haven't figured out what's going on between me and Sara yet. But I do know that I'm not ready to talk to her about my sister."

No, Sara would never understand what he'd done.

"What about the Lord?" Henry questioned.

"I thought I was listening to the Lord. That's how I ended up in Paradise."

"It seems trite to say I've been there, Ben. But I have. I want to encourage you to let the people who care for you in."

Clamping his jaw, Ben fought the overpowering emotions that pummeled him.

"Forgive yourself, Ben," Henry said softly.

"I'm not sure I can be forgiven," he murmured in response.

In an instant, Ben's own words cracked his carefully built walls. Suddenly everything came tumbling out. "You don't understand, sir. I left her alone in the hospital. She died. *My sister died, and I could have prevented it.*"

Ben bowed his head, unwilling to see what surely would be reflected in Henry Rhoades's eyes at the shameful admission.

Suddenly Henry was right next to him, with a hand on his shoulder. "Ben, there's nothing we've done that the Lord can't handle. Turn it over to him. I think you know in your head that you aren't to blame for your sister's death, any more than I am to blame for mine."

Ben took a slow, careful breath.

"The Lord can't help you the way He wants to, Ben. Not until you're ready to put it on the altar."

Lifting his head, Ben's eyes met Henry's gaze before the older man's gaze shifted to the photo on his desk of his sister and niece.

"Just think about it," he said.

"I will, sir."

"You aren't alone, son."

Ben nodded slowly, realizing for the first time that perhaps he wasn't.

Ben left Henry's office and walked the few blocks to the clinic. Entering by way of the side door, he peeked at the front desk, where the newly hired receptionist was sorting through boxes. Bypassing the lobby, he grabbed Mutt from his office and moved quickly down to the chapel.

The morning light streamed in through the stained-glass window behind the altar, illuminating the cross in a soft glow.

For a moment Ben stood mesmerized by the sight. "Okay, Lord," he whispered. "This is the best I can do right now. I'm giving it to You. Help me to be open to Your will."

Henry Rhoades's words echoed in Ben's mind as he looked up at the cross.

You aren't alone, son.

For the first time since Carolyn's death, Ben felt some of the burden lifting. He took a deep, cleansing breath.

Thank You, Lord.

When Mutt began to whine, Ben stepped

through the French doors outside to the garden and let the dog down.

A moment later his phone began to ring, and he answered without looking to see who it was—also without his usual hesitation.

"This is Ben."

He heard his mother's soothing voice. "Ben, I finally got you instead of your voice mail. Are you all right?"

"Mother? Yeah. I'm good. Better than I have been in a long time."

Ben paced back and forth across the stone path, stunned at this answer to prayer. The opportunity to make things right with his mother.

"We went to your condo, and you've apparently sublet. Where are you?"

"I'm in Paradise, Mother."

"Paradise?" She chuckled.

"Paradise, Colorado."

"Ah, God's country." He heard the smile in her voice.

"That's right," he said.

"Your father and I were quite worried. We'd like to see you. Spend time with you before our next trip."

"Where are you going this time?" he asked.

"Stateside. Appalachia."

"When do you leave?"

"First of October," she said.

"I'm assisting with a clinic that's scheduled to open in the middle of September. Why don't you and Dad come to Paradise?"

"We could do that. It's only a few weeks away."

"Yeah, I know, and I might even still be employed when you get here." He shrugged. "But it doesn't matter. Come anyhow. You'll like Paradise, and I'd like you to meet Sara Elliott."

"A special woman?" his mother asked.

"Sara is an amazing rural health doctor, and you know her mother, Amanda Rhoades."

"Oh, my. Amanda Rhoades's daughter? This is quite an incredible coincidence."

"Tell me about it."

"Ben, you're working in rural medicine?"

He laughed at her surprise. "Yeah, I guess I am."

"Wait until I tell your father."

"So you'll come down?" he asked.

"Yes. Of course. I'm excited, and I know your father will be, as well."

"I have a nice little cabin here. You can stay with me. It's sort of rustic, but it grows on you," he said.

His mother laughed. "Are you sure this is Ben?"

"Oh, yeah. It's me."

"Ben, you sound happy. That's wonderful."

"Thank you, Mother." He paused. "Thank you for not giving up on me."

"Ben, we all miss Carolyn, but right now it's you I'm thinking about. I miss you, Ben."

He bit back emotion. "I miss you, too, Mom."

"Talk to you soon," she said. "Remember that we love you."

"I love you, too. Say hi to Dad."

Ben tucked the phone away and rubbed a hand over his face. Henry Rhoades was a wise man.

He looked around for Mutt, and found the little dog running back and forth across the newly laid stone pavers, chasing a small butterfly. Ben followed the dog down the stone path to see the progress on the garden.

A foundation had been poured for the gazebo already, and several flower beds had been planted.

There was much more to be done. Ben recalled Henry Rhoades's vision for the area. Benches. A fountain. Trees and shrubs.

Ben was more determined than ever to make that vision a reality.

Suddenly everything became clear. He'd spent his whole life searching for something that money couldn't buy. He had come full circle in Paradise, and he'd learned so much from Sara and this town. His life was back on track, and he'd found his way home.

He glanced around again. There was work to do, and today was as good a day as any to take a ride into Monte Vista to get started.

He picked up his phone and called Sara. "Sara. It's Ben. Look, I know this is short notice, but I'm going to take the rest of the day off. I've got a few errands to run."

"Sure. Oh, and Ben, I found the rest of the accreditation paperwork and left it on your desk."

"Perfect. I'll get to it tomorrow."

"That's fine. So do you need any help with your errands?"

"I've got it covered." He paused. "And Sara?"

"Yes?"

"Thanks. For everything."

"Ben, are you okay? You sound like you're leaving or something."

"No. Just running errands."

"Good, because we have a lot to do in the next few weeks, and well, I'd miss you if you left."

"You know, I'd miss you, too." He was grateful she couldn't see the big goofy grin on his face.

Silence stretched for a moment.

"And Sara—did you ever give me directions to that church?"

"A block behind the café. Services are at ten on Sunday."

"Thanks."

"No problem."

He whistled for Mutt and walked back through the chapel, stopping only to look at the cross.

"Lord, I sure hope You're still saving a seat for me."

Chapter Twelve

Sara adjusted her Stetson and put on her best welcoming smile as she stood in front of the Elliott house, greeting guests and passing out the gift bags her father had insisted she put together. This was one of the few duties on the ranch she was uncomfortable with. Ask her to bale hay, ride fence lines or herd cattle, and she was ready and willing. But play hostess? She was completely out of her element and felt ridiculous pretending to be something she was not.

To her credit, she had given it her best and had been greeting her father's guests, most of the residents of Paradise, it seemed, for more than an hour to keep her father out of the sun.

"Sara, you've grown up to be just like your mother."

"Thank you, Mrs. Bodiker."

"Why, I can remember years ago when you were a little girl and your mother stood right where you are. The annual Elliott Ranch barbecue was her favorite event of the year. You're a lovely hostess, just like she was."

Sara smiled wanly and adjusted her silver bolo as the woman kept talking. She seriously doubted she was the hostess her mother was. Her mother took care of every detail of these events, from the caterer to the hayrides. Sara, on the other hand, was a delegator.

She could rationalize it away by claiming to be too busy with the clinic, because she was. And right now she'd rather be at the clinic working with Ben than here with all these people.

Looking up, she froze. Ben Rogers was walking up the long drive. Just thinking about him, and he appeared? There were dozens of guests pulling up and parking, on the grass and along the road, so how was it her internal antennae sensed the moment he arrived?

Suddenly the day looked promising, though the question remained.

Who had invited Ben? Her father?

Out of nowhere, a small sense of dread lodged in the back of her throat. Was Hollis Elliott manipulating her life again?

When Ben's crooked smile reached out to her, warming the frozen edges of her heart, she pushed the thought away.

Please, Lord, I'm trusting You to keep me safe.

Ben glanced around at the ranch with interest as he approached. Sara followed his gaze. The entire ranch had been decorated with streamers and balloons for the event. There was a face-painting station and donkey rides. A tent had even been set up with a small, country banjo band. Nothing was more festive than Elliott Ranch all dressed up for the annual community barbecue.

"Hi, Sara," someone said.

Sara returned the greeting, her attention never leaving Ben. Even in jeans and a T-shirt, he still managed to maintain that pressed-and-creased look. She had to admit to a strong urge to wrinkle him and muss his hair. That thought stopped her cold.

The last time she'd touched Ben had been a no-laughing matter. Her hand went to her mouth as she recalled their brief kiss.

"What's that expression on your face?" he asked as his foot landed on the first step of the porch.

"Ah, nothing." She gave him a weak smile as she thrust a gift bag at him. "Nice to see you."

"What's this?" He peeked into the bag.

"Oh, the usual. Elliott Ranch tchotchkes."

"Tchotchkes?" Ben raised his brows in question.

"You know, key chains, pens, whatnots with the ranch logo on them."

Ben pulled out a magnet in the shape of a bison. "Nice touch."

"Just what you always wanted, right?" Sara laughed and quickly covered her mouth as she saw her father approach.

"Dr. Rogers, good to see you again. We're glad you could make it."

Sara looked quizzically from her father to Ben.

Her father had invited Ben. Neither had said a word to her. She stiffened. Why the omission?

"Mr. Elliott." Ben reached out to shake her father's hand, though his gaze never left her. "Thank you for the invitation."

Sara chewed her lip, confused.

"Sara, show Ben around, would you? I've promised to show some of the neighbors the new toy in the garage. Unless you'd like to join us, Ben?"

"Actually, sir, I'd like to see the ranch." He turned to Sara. "If you don't mind."

Hollis nodded. "Sara would be happy to show you around. I hope you brought your appetite. We've got Elliott beef on that barbecue. The best in the valley."

"Yes, sir." Ben watched her father's retreating form and turned to Sara. "New toy?"

"You wanted to see it, didn't you?"

"Yeah, but don't I get points for resisting?"

"Do you need points?" Sara asked.

"When it comes to you, I think I might."

She blushed and waved a hand. "The tour starts this way. Look around you. All this will be mine someday. Whether I like it or not."

"I thought you loved the ranch."

"I do. I'm spoiled rotten. I take for granted that I can ride my horse for hours without seeing a soul. Or fish in the stocked pond we keep in the north forty."

"North forty? The ranch is that large?"

She sighed. "Larger than large. My father owns the land all the way from here to the base of that mountain."

"Wow. So what will happen to the ranch when your father retires?" Ben asked.

"I don't know. That word isn't in my father's vocabulary, so it's really a moot point. He won't even entertain a discussion on the topic. Eventually he'll have to let someone else take over the operation or sell." She shook her head. "I'd be happy with just the horses and a little land. But my father has a different connection to the land than I do." She turned to Ben. "Enough about me. Are you hungry?"

"I'm guessing I better be. But I'm not just yet." He smiled. "Nice of your father to invite me."

"So my father *did* invite you."

"You didn't know?" He glanced at her and frowned. "If this is uncomfortable for you…"

"No. Not at all. Why would it be? We're friends, right?"

"Right. I just thought maybe you might have a thing about coworkers and personal boundaries."

"It's more a father issue and personal boundaries."

Ben nodded slowly. "That much I figured."

"What did you think about my father? Does he look okay to you?" she asked.

"Truthfully, I didn't really notice."

"No?" She turned to him.

"One look at you, and I sort of forgot about your father."

Sara stopped and stared as pleasure warmed her. Heat crept up her face, and she knew with certainty that her ears were pink. "Ben, sometimes you say the most, well, honest things."

He shrugged. "Sorry."

"Don't be." She glanced down at her black jeans and crisp white Western shirt. "Thank you for the compliment."

"You're welcome."

"I like your boots," she said, noting with interest his well-worn Justins.

"Your father told me to wear them."

"He was testing you."

"Testing me?"

"If you have boots in your closet, you pass the first test."

Ben chuckled. "I'm going to try not to analyze that."

Sara adjusted her hat. "Do you ride?"

"Is that the second test?"

"Pretty much."

"I ride passably."

She raised a brow. "Are you serious?"

"You're surprised?" Ben laughed heartily, and she knew he was laughing at her.

"Let's just say yes, and leave it at that," Sara said.

"Still doing that, aren't you?" Ben asked.

"Hmm?" Her gaze followed the children running past them as she pointedly ignored his question.

"You know what I'm talking about. Jumping to conclusions," he said.

Sara lifted a shoulder. "It's the only way I can stay ahead."

"No. I think it's a defense mechanism. The only way you know to protect yourself," he returned.

"Perhaps." She acknowledged his remark and dismissed it lightly.

"And perhaps when it comes to testing people, you're more like your father than you want to admit."

"I'd have to say perhaps to that, as well."

He grinned.

"So, do you want to meet Rocky?"

Ben's eyes widened at the challenge. "Do you want me to meet Rocky?"

"Of course." She walked with purpose toward the barn door, stopping to scoop up a handful of feed on the way. She paused at the first stall. "Ben. Rocky."

Ben looked from Sara to the horse. "So Rocky really is a horse," he stated.

"Yes. I told you he was. What did you think?"

"To tell you the truth, the first time you mentioned him I figured he was some seven-foot-tall cowboy with six-pack abs. When you said he was a horse, I thought you were messing with me."

Sara laughed, unable to hide her amusement.

Ben held out a hand for the horse to inspect. When the high-spirited black-and-white gelding snorted, then nudged his hand, Ben reached up to scratch his ears.

"He likes you," she said.

"Yeah, animals, small children and old folks tend to like me. The jury is still out on the rest of the population."

Sara held out the feed to Rocky, who began to lick her palm. "Good boy."

When Sara glanced up, Ben was watching her. Her skin warmed beneath his gaze. "Up for a little ride?" she asked.

"Now? What about your guests?"

"You're a guest, Ben. Besides, I could use some air. I've been standing in the sun for over an hour. I was getting claustrophobic with all those people."

Ben laughed and stared at her.

Sara glanced away, because she knew exactly what he was thinking. She was more like him than she wanted to admit. She'd accused Ben of being a loner, and then she'd gone and admitted that what she really wanted was to retreat to someplace quiet.

But she'd invited him along. Did that qualify her as a loner, or just a woman who was dangerously close to losing her heart?

"Watch out," Ben called.

As Sara yanked on the reins and tried to avert the low-hanging branch, Rocky snorted in agitation and reared back.

Suddenly Sara was on the ground, shaking her head and blinking.

"Are you okay?" Ben asked. He dropped from his horse to the ground, adrenaline pumping, and began assessing her for neurological damage. "Let me see your pupils."

"Stop. I'm totally humiliated, but I'm fine. Help me up."

"No. Don't move," Ben said, sharper than he intended.

"I said I'm fine," Sara repeated, this time with a healthy dose of irritation in her voice.

He held out a hand and Sara grasped it, standing up. "Did you hit your head?" he asked.

"I've been riding a long time. I know how to fall. As usual, I landed hard on my dignity. Fortunately it's well padded."

"So you don't want me to call for a doctor? Or two?"

Sara paused and narrowed her eyes, then she started laughing. "And I used to think you were humorless."

"Me? Now that is funny."

She dusted twigs and dirt off her jeans.

"What happened back there?" Ben asked.

"I pulled back when I saw the branch, but Rocky got spooked. Must have been a snake or something in that underbrush."

"Hang on a minute. Let me see if I can find him." Ben walked down the path. No sign of Rocky, but he did find her hat. He walked slowly back to give Sara a few minutes to piece together her ego.

"Thanks." She dusted off the hat on her jeans.

"I didn't see Rocky."

Sara looked around and shrugged. "Give him a few minutes. He never wanders far."

"Your backside," Ben said.

"My what?" She tried to look over her shoulder. "Are you telling me I'm covered with dirt?"

He gave a reluctant nod.

"Oh, great," she moaned. "I can't go back to the party looking like I took a tumble with a cowboy."

Ben chuckled. "I like that. Your ego may be bruised, but mine is doing just fine."

Her mouth began to twitch at one corner as she tried to dust off her posterior.

"Um, you've got some stuff in your hair, as well," Ben said.

Sara pulled out her ponytail holder and shook her head. The long dark tresses waved around her head like a satin sheet. He stared, mesmerized by the sight.

"Better?"

Ben swallowed. "Uh, yeah." He stepped forward, and as if in slow motion, slid his fingers into her hair and pulled out a dried leaf. "Twig," he mumbled.

Their eyes connected.

Somehow the distance between them closed ever so slowly. Ben's hand slid to her smooth, long neck, then burrowed into her hair as he gently lifted her head toward him. By the time he leaned in to touch his mouth to hers, he was near dizzy.

For a brief moment he noticed that her lips

were soft and warm, tasting faintly of mint and vanilla. Then he was lost in the connection between them.

When it ended, Sara's eyes remained closed. "No," she protested from the circle of his arms.

"Sara," he whispered, gently pushing the hair away from her face.

Her lids fluttered open, and she smiled. "There's Rocky." She moved away from Ben and toward her horse.

They were silent as they walked their horses back to the barn.

"Sara, I..."

"Just let it go, Ben."

What did that mean? He was woefully ignorant when it came to woman-speak, but he figured she was trying to say she didn't want to talk about the kiss they'd just shared.

Finally Ben turned to her to try a different tact. "Do you think that sometime we could do something together besides work at the clinic?"

Her green eyes widened.

"I guess that's a no."

"No. I was just surprised."

"Why? I like you, Sara. To tell you the truth, it scares me how much I like you."

"I like you, too, Ben."

"So why not? We have a lot in common, and we certainly have some kind of chemistry going for us."

Sara stared at Ben as if seeing him for the first time. He knew it wasn't a good sign when she stepped back carefully.

"Suddenly you want to date me?" she asked.

He smiled. "Not so suddenly. Maybe suddenly I have the courage to say something."

She shook her head, and her eyes clouded with concern. "I don't know if that's such a good idea. You've become a very valuable friend to me. I don't want to jeopardize that friendship. And we've got a lot going on with the clinic—neither one of us should be focused on anything else right now."

He shoved his hands into his front pockets.

"And what will happen in September when one of us…you know."

"It's just a job, Sara. I thought people were more important than things to you."

"You're twisting my words around. Besides, I have a hard time reconciling your telling me it's just a job now with how angry and fiercely determined you were in July, especially when you found out Dr. Rhoades was my uncle."

Again she shook her head, this time more adamantly. "This is a no-win situation for us, Ben. You may say the job doesn't mean as much to you anymore, but what if I'm chosen? You'll always wonder if it was because I'm qualified, or because my father is Hollis Elliott. Eventually that would tear us apart."

"What about you, Sara?"

"Me?"

"There's something else going on here. You're afraid. Afraid of getting hurt."

She took a deep breath. "I think you should know exactly why I left Paradise two years ago."

"Okay."

She dropped the reigns and paced back and forth, wringing her hands. "I was engaged."

Ben raised a brow.

"This isn't easy to admit, but I was duped into believing my fiancé actually loved me. I'm obviously a poor judge of character."

Ben raised a brow. "The way I see it, you choose to see the best in people."

She released a bitter laugh. "That's a nice way of putting it. I wish that was true."

Again she paced.

"My fiancé was marrying me for my dowry. It's an old-fashioned term, but basically quite applicable here. My father promised him a partnership in the ranch if he'd court and marry his daughter. I fell for it, lock, stock and Elliott cattle."

Sara closed her eyes for a moment.

"I'm so sorry," Ben whispered. He stepped toward her, longing to wrap her in his arms and chase away her pain.

She stepped back.

"So we don't even get a chance?" he asked.

"We've become good friends. I don't want to risk that."

He didn't answer. In some ways she was so very much like her father. She thought she had all the answers.

Sara picked up Rocky's reigns again and started walking. Ben blinked as he followed her down the path and into the bright Colorado sunlight. He had been shot down in broad daylight. She certainly had a talent for getting to the point. And he thought that was his forte.

"How about some ribs?" Sara asked.

"Ribs?" His head was spinning, and she wanted ribs?

"Yes. Ribs and grilled corn on the cob, and Malla even made her famous potato salad. Do you know how many potatoes I had to peel to help her make enough potatoes for this crowd?"

She was babbling, and he wanted badly to let her off the hook, but he couldn't. His heart ached too much to even try.

"Orvis and Anna Carter are over there," Ben said. "Mind if I go say hi?"

"No, of course not. You know, there are a few things I should check on right now." She smiled a little too brightly. "I'm apparently acting hostess for this shindig."

"You did a great job, Sara. Your mother would be proud."

She inhaled sharply. "Everyone keeps saying that, but I can't help but feel like a poor replacement."

"Don't do that to yourself," Ben said. "The

Lord has a special calling for your life. Stop regretting everything else."

Silence stretched like a taut rope between them.

Finally Sara met his gaze. "You know what, Ben? You're right. You aren't the man you were when you arrived in Paradise."

"I'll take that as a good thing." He walked toward the smoking grills. "You're right—I better grab some of those ribs before they're all gone."

She nodded, almost sadly.

Ben took a deep breath, not seeing anything as he walked away from Sara. Suddenly everything had shifted. It wasn't just about the clinic director position. No, things had become much more complicated. When had he fallen for her? He couldn't pinpoint the moment. But there it was.

Now he had to ask himself if he really wanted a future in Paradise without Sara Elliott.

Chapter Thirteen

"If I were paranoid, which I'm not, I'd say you were avoiding me," Ben commented as he poured coffee into his cup on Tuesday morning. After spending the weekend doing nothing but thinking, he was determined to get their friendship back on track after the disaster at the barbecue. But Monday he'd barely glimpsed her passing his office, and then she disappeared for the day. Sara's head popped up from around the refrigerator door. "My father's cardiologist is in Denver. So if driving four hours to Denver yesterday was avoiding you, then yes, I'm definitely avoiding you."

"Why didn't you tell me you were going? I would have been happy to go with you."

"I needed time to think, Ben."

Time to think? Think about what? That kiss on Saturday? Or maybe how she'd shot him down and left him for dead?

He paused and chastised himself. This wasn't about him; it was about her father.

Either way, it didn't sound good.

"So what did the cardiologist have to say?" he asked.

"Well, he opened with the usual chastisements, but my father didn't take in a word. He thinks he's God and a medical professional rolled into one." Sara released a frustrated sigh.

"And I thought only doctors had God complexes," Ben said.

"Ben, this is serious. My father has more cardiac arrhythmia than I want to think about, along with cardiomegaly issues related to his congestive heart failure. By ignoring his condition and not following his medication regime, he's a ticking bomb ready to go off."

"I'm sorry you have to deal with this," Ben said.

"Thanks. I guess part of me is feeling guilty for not being on top of things. I thought he was just giving me smack talk when he said he wasn't going to take his pills."

"You can't blame yourself," Ben said.

"Yes, actually, I can. I think he's given up."

"Maybe he's depressed. I'm not telling you anything you don't already know. But it's not unusual for depression to follow chronic illness, and then the cycle just repeats itself. The depressed patient is much more likely to become a noncompliant patient."

She stared at him, her eyes widening. "You know, you're absolutely right. I'm so close to the problem, I can't even see objectively to make the right decisions. If it had been one of my patients, I would have picked up on that immediately."

"So what did the heart doc recommend?" Ben asked.

"A pacemaker. Apparently he recommended it weeks ago, and my father already vetoed that plan of care."

"That doesn't make sense. Why?"

Sara quoted her father. "If the good Lord wanted me to have a pacemaker, He would have given me one." She shook her head. "This would be amusing if he wasn't my father. This time his money can't buy him what he needs—a large dose of common sense. To make matters worse, the cardiac practice has concluded the same thing. They don't care how much money he has. When the name Hollis Elliott is spoken, they all run—in the other direction. He's been fired as a patient."

"They fired your father? Okay, I don't think I've fired a patient yet."

"I feel fortunate that neither have I." She gave an impatient nod of agreement. "So here's where we stand. The cardiologist has signed off his case and turned his care back over to his primary-care physician, who has too many compliant patients to deal with one who so flagrantly is not."

Ben blinked. He'd had his share of difficult patients himself, but it seemed Hollis was setting the bar higher. "Okay," he said. "So what are you going to do?"

"I guess I'll call my uncle and see if he has any suggestions—and then I better step up the prayers."

"Good idea. When in doubt, ask Henry and God."

They shared a laugh. Sara glanced around

the room, and Ben followed the direction of her gaze.

The kitchen was starting to show signs of life since the new office staff had been hired, from the plant on the table to the cheery framed prints on the wall. "What did I miss around here yesterday?" she asked.

"Not much," Ben said. "They striped the parking lot and gave us our own spaces."

Sara glanced out the window at the view of the parking lot. "I've been meaning to ask you where your Land Rover is," Sara said.

"It's not out there?"

She frowned. "You know it isn't."

Ben took a sip of coffee as he considered how to change the subject. He swallowed. "Did I mention that we lost the bids for those primary-care docs?"

"What? Not both of them? We open in three weeks! We can't open without doctors."

"I don't understand why we're getting such a poor response to the package we offer," Ben said.

"Apparently, the appeal of year-round altitude sickness, a population of seventeen hundred and nineteen, and a stunning low-end base salary isn't enough to dazzle the big-city doctors. Who would have thought?"

"What are you talking about? I think this is a great place to practice medicine," he said.

"But you aren't the norm," Sara returned.

"I'm sure you meant that as a compliment."

"I meant you and I have a heart for Paradise," she said. "Finding physicians who feel the same way isn't going to be easy."

Ben nodded.

"Ask your father about the stats on this," Sara said. "He'll agree that recruitment and retention of physicians for rural medicine is a constant struggle. Most physicians want to work in a setting that offers more perks, including time off. Rural medicine practitioners have a higher rate of burnout because of this. It's a vicious cycle."

"So what did the head hunter recommend?" Ben asked.

"The impossible. Going to the board and asking for more money." She sank into a chair. "That isn't going to happen."

"Cheer up. If worse comes to worst, you and I will run the show," he said.

"Well, I can't say I'd really mind," Sara said

with a lift of her shoulder. "I told you I miss direct patient care."

Ben shook his head. "You're in Paradise competing with me for a position you're ambivalent about, and yet you're willing to change your entire life to do what you don't want to do." He pinned her with a direct gaze. "Do I have that correct?"

"My father is sick. I can't disappoint him now. That's the bottom line." She got up and started down the hall.

"This is crazy," Ben said, trailing after her. "It's your life."

"I can't talk about this anymore, Ben." She glanced at the lobby, stopping so suddenly he nearly ran into her.

"Whoa, careful."

"Bitsy Harmony is in the lobby. Do you want to hide?"

"No, it's okay. She's, ah, helping me with some planting."

"You have Bitsy Harmony planting for you?" Sara tapped the side of her head with her palm. "I think I'm having some auditory impairment. I thought I heard you say…"

"Yeah, I did say that. Look, you said they

needed a project, and I was getting tired of planning my entire life around hiding from the Ladies' Auxiliary. So I decided to be proactive."

Sara looked at him like he was a foreign object. "Proactive? Ben, you're an amazing guy."

"Thanks." So why did he feel like he'd just told a fib? He hadn't lied. Bitsy was doing planting for him. Just not at his house.

"I have only one question," Sara said.

"What's that?"

"How does she carry those geraniums and petunias on her Harley?"

"You're just full of sass this morning," Ben said, giving her a slow stare.

She smiled sweetly. "You seem to bring out the best in me."

Ben shook his head. "No. I think I just bring out the real Sara in you, and to tell you the truth, I like her."

She looked up at him. "So does that mean you and I are okay?" she asked.

Relieved to hear her words, Ben released a breath. "Sara, we're fine. I don't want to lose your friendship. I'm sorry if I overstepped on Saturday."

"You didn't. I just… I guess I'm just not ready."

"That's okay." He smiled. "But maybe you could let me know when you are."

Her face turned pink as she nodded.

"I better go see my gardener," Ben said.

Sara's laughter followed him as he jogged out to the lobby.

"Bitsy."

"Dr. Rogers, we have a problem," Bitsy said. She clutched her purse and tote bag to her side.

He gently took her elbow and led her to the conference room.

"I only have a few minutes," she said. "I have to get back to the sheriff's office before he makes another cup of caffeinated mud without permission."

Ben opened his mouth and then closed it. He had learned right away that when interacting with the Paradise Ladies' Auxiliary, it was good protocol not to ask questions if you really didn't want to know the answers. Instead he tried to keep them focused at all times.

"What sort of problem?" he finally asked.

"Hollis Elliott showed up on Saturday."

"In the chapel garden?"

"Yep. I was spreading mulch and suddenly there he was, big as life with that Stetson on his head, and blowing steam like an out-of-control train."

"What exactly did he say?"

"He said he wasn't going to spend any more of his money on a garden if his daughter wasn't going to be clinical director."

"Bitsy, Hollis isn't paying for the garden."

She frowned. "He's not?"

"No, and I'm sorry he bothered you. Trust me, I'll take care of the situation. Immediately."

"I don't know if you can, Dr. Rogers," she said with a shake of her head. "He was pretty bossy, throwing around threats like they were pennies in a fountain."

"I can and will handle Hollis Elliott."

"Dr. Rogers, if you don't mind my asking, exactly who is funding the garden?"

Ben shoved his hands into his pockets. "Well Bitsy, the truth is, I am."

Bitsy's blue eyes crinkled at the corners, and a smile slowly spread across her face.

"You'll keep that information under your bun, right?"

She touched her hand to the knot at the top of her head. "I surely will. But I can hardly believe you got one over on Hollis, and he doesn't even know it."

Ben fought back a laugh. "That's okay. He doesn't need to know everything."

"You're so right, Dr. Rogers. You are so right."

"So how *is* the garden coming along?" he asked.

"We're right on schedule. The gazebo will be painted on Saturday." She released a wistful sigh. "Oh, it's just beautiful. The perfect place for a wedding."

"Did the benches arrive yet?"

"Not yet."

"I'll call and check on them."

"What about the problems with the sprinkler?"

"All fixed. Now we're waiting for Orvis's nephew to hook up the bubbler on the pond and finish the electric connection on the fountain."

"That's just great. Good thing Orvis has a big family. Electricians, plumbers and carpenters. I really owe him, big time."

"You know Orvis is just saying thank you because you saved his life. That man has a lot to live for. So don't worry about paybacks. Just let him help you."

Ben nodded, realizing Bitsy was right. Orvis Carter could teach Hollis Elliott a thing or two about being grateful for the blessings the Lord gives, and appreciating each day.

"When do we get to tell everyone about the garden?" she asked.

"Open house and the grand opening are less than three weeks away. I can hardly believe how fast time has passed."

"It tends to do that when you've got your heart and your hands working in the right place," she said.

"I guess so."

Bitsy nodded and picked up her purse and tote from the table. "You're getting your roots deep into this town, Dr. Rogers. Hope you don't have plans to move anytime soon. You might find you can't."

"No worries, Bitsy. I want to stick around Paradise. At least through September."

"Longer, I hope. You're good for this town."

"This town is good for me," he murmured.

As Bitsy walked away, Ben found that he actually believed those words, now more than ever.

Chapter Fourteen

"Mr. Elliott, thanks for seeing me on such short notice."

"Have a seat." His voice boomed out with a hard edge.

Ben sat, but he kept his eye on the rancher who sat behind the large desk. Sara was right. Something was more than just a little off with her father. Hollis's physical deterioration was obvious.

There was a notable unhealthy pallor to his face, and Ben detected a slight shortness of breath and wheezing when he spoke. Ben glanced quickly at Hollis's hands folded on the desk. Dusky nail beds. The man was in congestive heart failure.

Ben regrouped. This wasn't the time for

a strong defense. He needed to keep Hollis calm, and perhaps he could reason with him.

"Sir, I understand you stopped by the chapel garden on Saturday?"

"What of it? I want to see the hole my money is being buried in."

"Mr. Elliott, not a penny of your money has been used for the memorial chapel."

Hollis's eyes narrowed to glittering slits as he leaned forward like a hawk about to attack. There was no mercy in his face. "You're lying. You asked for my permission."

Ben swallowed the retaliatory response that rose up in his throat. He'd keep calm, and maybe Hollis would, as well. "Sir, I asked your permission to name the memorial garden after your wife. I didn't solicit funds."

There was a long pause, and the man behind the desk appeared confused. "How are you paying for the landscaping?"

"I'm funding the garden project."

"You?" Hollis slowly shook his head. "I want you to know I've earned every one of these gray hairs on my head. I'm no fool."

Confused, Ben looked at Hollis Elliott.

"Nobody does anything unless he stands to gain something from the effort."

"I don't agree, sir." Ben said. "Your wife is the perfect example."

Hollis's eyes widened a fraction in stunned surprise at the quick rebuttal.

"Amanda Rhoades-Elliott was known for her altruism and dedication. She inspired my own parents."

The kind words bounced off Hollis Elliott. He didn't want to hear them. It was obvious he was looking for a fight. Ben refused to satisfy him.

"Why are you here, Dr. Rogers?"

"To kindly ask you not to harass the Ladies' Auxiliary. They're working on the garden with no compensation, and I don't want them to feel threatened."

"Hollis Elliott doesn't harass."

"Good, then we agree." He stood to leave.

"What exactly is your interest in Sara?"

Ben turned back, surprised. "Excuse me?"

"You heard me. I don't want you leading her on for your own professional gain."

Hollis Elliott was baiting him. Ben paused

and took a deep, steadying breath against the slanderous remark.

Choose your words carefully.

"Sir, I'm not in the habit of discussing my personal affairs with others."

"Others? I'm her father, and I won't have her career or her emotions jeopardized."

"I can assure you that I, too, have Sara's best interests in mind. I have no intention of jeopardizing her career or her feelings. I've been totally upfront with her about my goals here in Paradise."

"You can assure me?" Hollis shook his head as if mocking him. "What happens when the director is chosen?"

"Sara and I will deal with that in September."

"I won't let her get hurt again. She'll leave Paradise if that happens."

In that moment, the man across from him seemed less formidable. Ben saw Hollis Elliott as simply a father, afraid of losing his only child.

"I care a great deal about Sara. You have my word that I won't intentionally hurt her."

"If you cared about Sara, then you'd withdraw your interest in the clinical director job."

Stunned that he was resorting to putting him in this position, Ben clenched his jaw. "Sir, you mentioned being upfront. I wonder if you've been upfront with your daughter?"

"I don't know what you're talking about," Hollis returned.

"I'm talking about your health. You've refused a pacemaker, and you've been noncompliant with your medication," Ben said.

"I don't need any fool electronic gadget put inside of me."

"That's not what your daughter tells me."

"Did she also tell you that I like people to stay out of my business?"

"Sir, your daughter is very concerned about your health."

Hollis paused, once again his sharp eyes assessing. "You look like a man of your word, Dr. Rogers."

"Always."

"Then I'll offer you this. I'll comply with my medical regime if you withdraw from the director position."

Ben froze. "You can't be serious."

"Oh, I'm more than serious. I'd bet my life I'm very serious."

Ben was silent. *Lord give me the words. Show me what to do.*

"Do you know what it's like to lose someone you love?" Hollis said the words quietly.

"Yes, sir. I do."

"Then you know that sometimes you do whatever you deem necessary to hold on to what you have left."

Suddenly the door to Hollis Elliott's study burst open.

"What's going on?" Sara asked, looking from Ben to her father, searching for a clue to the tension that filled the room.

"Just talking business with your father," Ben said.

"Business? What sort of business?" If she sounded frantic, it was because that was exactly how she felt right now. This was the second time Ben and her father were meeting without her knowledge. What business could the two of them possibly have to discuss, and without her? The possibility terrified her.

"I was encouraging your father to get the pacemaker."

"What?" She pushed her hair back from her face and stared at Ben. "Why would you do that? I shared that information with you in confidence."

"You and I can talk later, Sara. Right now, I think I should leave."

"Make sure you think long and hard on what we discussed, Dr. Rogers."

"Oh, I will, sir. You can bet I will."

The conversation between the two men swirled around her, yet she still stood in the dark and more confused than ever.

Sara followed Ben to the front porch, barely keeping up with his long strides. "Ben? Are you seriously leaving without explaining what's going on?" she asked.

"I have to go."

His voice was flat, and he wouldn't look at her. Suddenly Sara was very frightened. Something was wrong. Very wrong. The private, detached Ben who had arrived in Paradise weeks ago, hurting, she understood. This indifference she couldn't reach.

"No, Ben. Don't go. I want to know exactly what you two were discussing."

"I told you. Your father's medical condition."

"How could you break my confidence, and to my father. My father of all people?"

Finally he met her gaze, and she saw the emotion he tried to hide. "I did it because I care about you."

He opened his car door.

Confused, she looked at the compact car and then at Ben. "Where's your Land Rover?"

"Does it really matter?"

"Ben," she pleaded. "Don't go. We have to talk about this."

"Talk to your father. I'm sure he can answer any concerns you have."

Concerns? She had much more than concerns warring in her mind and spirit right now. She leaned against a porch pillar and watched the car until it disappeared from view. Had she learned anything in two years? This time she wasn't just going to let things happen.

She was the daughter of Amanda Rhoades-

Elliott, and this time around she was going to fight for what she wanted.

Ben sat in his backyard with a tall glass of water. Mutt sat next to him. "So how'd you like to see Denver, Mutt?"

Mutt refused to answer.

A car door slammed, and Ben braced himself for what was surely coming. He heard a rattling noise right before Sara walked into the backyard.

"I thought you had an appointment," she said, irritation warm on her face.

He shrugged. "I did. I promised Mutt I'd be home early." She frowned, her lips a tight line.

"How did you get through that gate?"

"I kicked it."

"Nice." Ben nodded in admiration. "Water?"

"No, thanks. This isn't exactly a social visit."

"No? What exactly is it?"

"It's me asking you to assure me that my father isn't manipulating my life again, like he did two years ago."

"Your engagement?"

Sara nodded, her eyes pleading with him.

He paused. "You don't think that's why I was talking to your father today, do you?"

"I don't know what to think. I just know I can't do it again."

"Sara, I've always been honest with you."

"Then tell me what you and my father discussed."

"I told you."

"No. There's something else, and I know it. You're a terrible liar."

Ben stood and walked over to where Sara stood. He gently pushed the hair away from her face. "Your father would never have to pay me to care about you."

A tremor slid over him as his gaze met hers.

"Then please," Sara whispered. "Don't let me be a fool again."

He stepped back from her, and away from temptation, knowing what he had to do if he really loved Sara. "I've been thinking a lot about what you said at the barbecue."

"Oh," she groaned. "That's a huge mistake. Never think a lot about anything I say after I've been kissed."

Ben chuckled. "I'm just saying that I think you were right."

"Right? I wasn't right. What I was was confused and afraid of what I felt for you."

"You raised some valid points. It probably is best for both of us if we keep things professional for now."

She stepped back as though she'd been slapped. Her eyes rounded. "You're telling me to stop caring for you? Is this some sort of payback?"

"Of course not. I'm just saying that you made sense. The clinic directorship stands between us. Let's wait until that dust settles, and then we can revisit the topic of us."

"Revisit the topic?" Sara stiffened as she moved from confusion straight into anger. Maybe that was a good thing. It would protect her from what he had to do.

"You know what I'm trying to say," Ben finally said, a weary resignation settling over him.

"Fine, Dr. Rogers," she said, blinking back moisture.

Ben shook his head, knowing he was messing up the best thing that had happened to him in a very long time.

"It doesn't have to be like this, Sara. We can still be friends."

"As I recall, I was the one who first said that to you, back in July."

"And you were right."

"Well, being right isn't very satisfying after all," she said.

"Sara."

Mutt whimpered.

Sara took a step toward the dog, then turned away with a sigh.

He heard the gate clang as she left. and shook his head. Could the means possibly justify the end?

Mutt whined again, and he leaned down to rub him behind the ears. "It's okay, boy. It's okay."

Except it really wasn't okay.

Hollis Elliott hadn't just manipulated Sara this time, he'd manipulated everything. Could the Lord reach the Cattle King of Paradise Valley and untangle this mess? Ben hoped so.

Chapter Fifteen

Sara lifted her head as she heard the familiar sound of Uncle Henry wheeling down the clinic hallway. She was pretty sure he spent more time at the clinic these days than he did at the hospital. The closer they got to the opening, the more time he spent checking equipment and reviewing documentation.

"Sara?" He peeked his head into her office and smiled. As usual, his tufts of hair were slightly mussed, and his tie was askew.

Sara smiled, and realized it was the first time she'd smiled all day. She'd barely slept last night after her conversation with Ben. Over and over again, she had replayed his words, trying to figure out how to make things right. She'd come into the office earlier than usual, hoping they'd have a chance to talk, but it was almost noon and Ben wasn't in yet.

"Hi, Uncle Henry. I was just about to call you." She glanced at the clock again. "I haven't seen Ben all morning. Did he happen to leave a message with you?"

"He did. In fact, he came to see me this morning."

Sara frowned, her gaze searching her uncle's face for a clue to what could be going on. *Where was Ben?*

"Is everything okay?" she asked.

"I'm confident it will be," he returned with a smile. "Do you have a moment, dear?"

"Uncle Henry, not only are you my boss, but you're my favorite uncle. Of course I have a minute."

He chuckled. "Then I won't point out that I happen to be your only uncle."

"What's up, only and favorite uncle?"

"I'd like to show you something," he said with a wry smile.

She gave him a sideways glance. "Did I forget to order something?"

"No." He shook his head and laughed. "Follow me."

She closed the file on her desk and let him lead the way down the hall to the doorway on the other side of the chapel.

"Uncle Henry, we're not supposed to go out there." She pointed to the "Construction—Do Not Enter" sign posted on the door.

"Oh, you can take that down, Sara. I put that sign up, but it's all completed now."

"What is?"

"Hold the door, Sara, and I'll show you."

She shaded her eyes as they stepped outside. Focusing, Sara stopped and gasped. A garden. A lovely fenced-in garden, with walkways and niche areas beneath trees where stone benches invited meditation. An old-fashioned gazebo stood in the center. All along the fence, splashes of bright wildflowers had begun to bloom. More flowers followed the stone pathway, circling a charming little pond whose fountain bubbled water into the quiet of the garden.

"Uncle Henry, what is this?"

"This is the Amanda Rhoades-Elliott Memorial Garden."

Sara swallowed, overwhelmed with emotion. Her eyes welled up, finally overflowing. "Why didn't you tell me?" she sniffed.

"I am telling you," he chuckled.

"But how?"

"Sara, Ben did this. All of it."

Stunned, she whirled around to look at her uncle. "Ben?"

"Yes. Ben. He asked your father's permission to name the garden after your mother. I instructed him to ask your father for funding, but apparently he wisely chose to ignore my instructions. Instead he took the project on himself. He's quite determined and strongwilled, that young man."

"But what do you mean, took it on himself?"

"Ben has quite a few friends in Paradise."

"Does he?" she asked with a small smile. Huh—the man who likes to be alone has quite a few friends. How about that?

"Orvis and his sons did a large portion of the work. The Paradise Ladies' Auxiliary is responsible for the landscape design and planting."

"Planting?" She shook her head, remembering Bitsy Harmony in the lobby last week. Proactive, he had said.

"Who paid for all this?" she asked, more confused than ever.

"Ben did."

Her eyes flew open. "He sold the Land Rover."

"Yes. He did."

"Uncle Henry." She looked down at her uncle. "Why did he do this?"

"I believe he did it because he loves you, and because he understands your loss."

Tears began to flow unchecked, and she lowered herself to a bench.

"I'm such an idiot. I thought he sold-out to my father."

"On the contrary. He sold-out *for* you."

She wiped her face with her fingers. "What do you mean?"

"Ben resigned today."

Sara shook her head. "No!"

Hadn't she learned anything in two years? Once again, everything in her life in Paradise was falling apart, and she didn't know how to fix it.

Lord, show me Your ways.

* * *

Ben slipped into the clinic's side door. Sara rarely detoured from her schedule. Right now she'd be at lunch, eating a salad with a glass of tea at The Prospector. She'd keep a bag of almonds in her briefcase for later, and then she'd offer him half.

He was going to miss those almonds.

He was going to miss *everything* about her.

If he was quick, he could empty out his desk before she got back. He placed a box on his desk and started shoving stuff inside. In the bottom drawer, he pulled out the paperwork that came with his stethoscope and tossed it in the box. It would go to the E.R. doc at the Paradise Hospital whom he'd sold it to.

As he opened another drawer, a loud thud echoed from the lobby. He lifted his head and listened, but heard nothing else.

Most likely a delivery.

Ben kept grabbing papers from his desk and neatly stacking them in a folder for Sara. He took a deep breath. He hated to leave her with the rest of the accreditation paperwork, but it was all going to be hers soon anyway.

Heavy footsteps moved at a sluggish pace down the hall. Not Sara. But who?

Ben looked up at the sound of raspy, wheezy breathing.

"Hollis."

Hollis Elliott leaned against the doorjamb, his Stetson shading his craggy face, which was gray and clammy beneath the office lighting. And then he started going down, sliding to the floor.

Ben reached him and eased the older man onto the floor, until he was half sitting and half lying against his desk. Wheezing was audible. No stethoscope needed. Yanking up Hollis's pant legs, Ben evaluated the edema.

Plus three. Pitting.

"I…I don't…I don't feel well," Hollis puffed.

That was an understatement. The man was going under—and fast.

"Sara? Is Sara here?"

"No. Sorry, sir, you're just going to have to put up with me saving your life today. We can argue about it later. Okay?"

Ben raced into the exam room and grabbed the code cart with force, wheeling it down the hall as he dialed 9-1-1, putting them on speakerphone.

"This is Dr. Ben Rogers. I'm only two blocks away at the Paradise Clinic. We need an ambulance ASAP. Male. Caucasian. Sixty years. History of cardiac arrhythmia, myo-cardial infarction and congestive heart fail-ure. Presenting with exacerbated shortness of breath and worsening bilateral edema."

"Sorry, doctor, the only ambulance is ten minutes out at an automobile accident with fatalities. I don't even have a patrol car avail-able to assist. Can you bring him in?"

"I'll try. Make sure they're waiting for me."

"Yes, doctor."

He shoved the cart into his office.

Defibrillator.

Ben glanced at the top of the cart where the equipment should have been, then realized they didn't have a defibrillator yet.

Better not need one.

Ben pulled out tubing and a mask and opened up the oxygen on the portable tank. "Let's get this mask on you, Hollis."

Opening another drawer, Ben grabbed the

blood-pressure cuff and stethoscope. Hollis grunted.

"Just talking to myself, Hollis."

Blood pressure one hundred over twenty. Pulse eighty and irregular. Bilateral lung stridor on auscultation.

"Chest pain, Hollis?"

Sara's father shook his head.

"Nausea?"

"No," he said, his voice muffled through the mask.

"That's good. That's very, very good."

Ben fumbled in the drawers for a rubber tourniquet and opened the medication drawer.

"Hollis, I'm going to give you a little furosemide to ease the fluid accumulation, then we're going to grab that wheelchair in the lobby, put you in my car and get you to the emergency room."

"Thank. You." Hollis panted the words.

Ben noted the first positive sign. Hollis was still short of breath, but his breathing was slightly less labored.

"Don't waste your breath talking." Ben hunched down and looked the older man in the eyes. "Just relax. Concentrate on breathing. Everything is under control. You're going to be all right. I won't let anything happen to you. Got it?"

Hollis nodded, and Ben saw relief flicker in the older man's eyes.

"Good, now grab my arm if you have chest pain or if you feel faint."

Ben began to quietly pray, loud enough for Hollis to hear as he drew the furosemide up into a syringe. The feisty rancher could use a few prayers. Besides, they both needed assurance that the Lord was in control of the situation.

"Father, I thank You for guiding me as I help Hollis. Protect him as we head to the emergency room. Give me strength and wisdom and Lord, please, get me into that emergency room without incident. I know I can do it this time with Your help. Amen."

Chapter Sixteen

"I already asked him. Ben refuses to re-submit his paperwork for the clinic director position," Henry Rhoades said. He looked pointedly across the hospital room at his brother-in-law.

"What do you want me to do about it?" Hollis growled, adjusting his bed linens.

"I don't know, but you better think of something. Sara withdrew her application, as well. I've put up with a lot from you over the years, Hollis, but this time I've had it."

Hollis glanced at his daughter. "You withdrew your application?"

"I did." She grinned, because she knew that for the first time in her life, she had the upper hand with her father.

"The clinic is scheduled to open in two weeks, Sara," her uncle said, perplexed. "We've come this far, and now we are without a director and without physicians."

"No, Uncle Henry, that isn't quite true," Sara countered.

"I'm confused," he said.

"Here's what's going to happen." She nodded to Hollis. "My father will have his pacemaker implanted next week, because he promised to be compliant with his medical regime if Ben resigned from the clinic director position. Right, Dad?"

Hollis nodded slowly, with resignation.

"Thank you for being a man of your word. I knew I could count on you." She smiled and patted his hand before turning to her uncle.

"Uncle Henry, the clinic makes you happy. Very happy, in fact. It's okay to admit it. You spend more time in the clinic these days than the hospital. The clinic director position was yours from the beginning. You've given the hospital twenty-five years. It's time for something new, don't you think? And I bet Gabriella would love to come and work with you at the clinic."

Henry's owl eyes grew even wider behind his glasses. He grinned. "I do believe you may be right. On all counts, my dear. That's a splendid idea."

"I am right, Uncle Henry. I'm actually right a lot of the time. The problem is that I fail to listen to my heart, and instead I second-guess everything."

"That still doesn't solve the problem of our physician shortage," Henry said.

"That part is easy," Sara said. She picked up her briefcase. "I have to go and convince Ben that he and I are the new clinic rural-care physicians."

"Why not director?" her father asked.

"Director was your dream, Dad. Not mine. So unless you want to go to medical school, let's give the job to Uncle Henry. Besides, this way I'll have more time to spend helping you at the ranch."

She leaned over the bed to kiss her father. "Behave yourself while I'm gone. No arguing with the nurses. I gave them my phone number."

"So am I hearing you correctly? You're

staying in Paradise?" her father asked, his craggy face hopeful.

"Yes. I am staying in Paradise. We're going to find a way to keep my dreams, and yours, alive. But we're going to have to compromise. Okay?"

"Yes, Sara," Hollis said. "I'm grateful to be alive and grateful that Ben was at the clinic when I needed a doctor."

"Ben Rogers isn't just a good doctor, he's a Godly man. A good man."

"What are you waiting for, then?" her uncle asked. "Go tell him that."

"I'm going, I'm going."

Sara gave her father and uncle a little wave as she walked out of the hospital room. Two men down, one to go. Now all she had to do was convince the man she loved to stay with her in Paradise.

He's gone.

Sara fought the panic that threatened to choke her. Less than twenty-four hours, and Ben had already packed up and left for Denver? Without even as much as a forwarding address.

Who had Flora rented the cabin to? A huge silver RV filled the driveway.

She leaned back against the seat and bit her trembling lip. This wasn't how it was supposed to end.

Then she heard a dog bark. *Mutt.*

He left Mutt?

Sara got out of her car. "Mutt? Here, boy! Where are you?"

The barking was coming from inside the RV. Sara yanked open the door at the same time someone pushed it open from the inside. Sara flew across the gravel drive.

"Don't move. I'll call a doctor."

"That's not funny, Ben." She slowly opened her eyes, savoring the sight of him.

Mutt trotted over and licked her face.

"Mutt. I missed you," she said.

"What about me?" Ben asked.

She narrowed her eyes and looked at him again. There was a smudge of grease on his cheek, and his hair was all messed up.

"You're all dirty." She sighed. "And you have two heads."

"And I think you have a concussion," he said.

"I'm kidding," Sara said. She started to sit up.

"No. Don't move. You might have a spinal injury—your neck."

Sara held out her hand as Ben continued to spout neurological warnings.

"Good grief, I'm fine. Let me be the judge of my neuro status."

Ben pulled her to her feet. For a moment he held on to her hand and stared at her, his face unreadable. Finally he released her and took a pained breath.

"What are you doing here, Sara?" he asked.

"I'm going job hunting, and I thought you might want to go with me."

Ben narrowed his eyes. "Job hunting? What about the clinic?"

"I decided it wouldn't be any fun without you. So I promoted my uncle to director and cleaned out my desk."

"You quit?"

She nodded.

Ben ran a hand over his face as he took in her words. "And your father?"

"He's busy scheduling his pacemaker."

"That's good news, right?"

"It is." She smiled. "Thank you. For everything."

"I didn't do anything."

"Ben, you did everything. I don't think I've ever known anyone so selfless and giving."

He shook his head and grimaced. "Please don't give me too much credit. The Lord led me to Paradise for another chance because I was wholly selfish. My sister died because of my selfishness."

"Ben, if God can forgive you, why can't you forgive yourself?"

"You're right. He gave the ultimate sacrifice, and I need to remember that." Ben glanced away, then his gaze met hers. "I guess it's just that I don't want you to see me as anything other than what I am."

"What? A sinner who is saved by grace?" She touched his arm. "Yes, I'm one, too."

He shook his head at her words. "Thanks, Sara," he said.

"Ben, can we just start over?"

Hope flared in his dark eyes, and he slowly nodded. "Yeah," he said. "I'd like that."

"Then how long do you think we need to wait before I can tell you I'm in love with you?" Sara asked, her head cocked in question.

Ben coughed. "Sorry." He choked out the word. "Swallowed my gum."

"Do you need the Heimlich?" she asked with a laugh.

"I'm fine. I just thought you said…" His voice trailed off as his gaze met hers.

Sara reached up and rubbed a spot of grease from his cheek. "What's this?" she asked as she examined the black smudge on her fingers.

"I'm working on the RV."

"What are you going to do with an RV?"

"I sort of bought it before I resigned."

She frowned. "I'm missing something in this equation."

"This is—I mean, was—our mobile clinic."

Sara's eyes rounded with delight. "Oh, Ben—the mobile clinic!"

"Yeah. Think it will work?"

"Only if you and I are driving it," she said.

"My toy. I get to drive," Ben countered.

"I might get a turn if you'll consider working at the clinic with me."

"I don't think we can do that again," he said.

"I'm talking about as staff physicians."

"Staff physicians?" His brows raised.

"Remember, there is the appeal of year-round altitude sickness, a population of seventeen hundred and nineteen, and the stunning low-end base salary."

"Yeah. That is hard to resist," he admitted. "But I'd probably want to do it for the perks."

"What perks?" Sara asked.

Ben pulled her close into the circle of his arms. "Working side-by-side with the woman I love."

Sara gulped, surprised and delighted to hear the words tumble from his lips.

"You love me?" she asked.

"How could I not? You put up with me when I was an emotional mess."

Sara sighed. "Do you think you could possibly kiss me?" she asked.

He looked down at his shirt and jeans. "But I'm all dirty."

"I love you just the way you are, Dr. Rogers." She wrapped her arms around his neck and pulled his head down to hers until his lips touched her mouth.

"My mother would have loved you," Sara whispered when she was done kissing him.

Ben took a deep breath, and his eyes became moist. "Sara, my sister would have loved you."

"God is so good," Sara said. "He heals the broken-hearted and binds up their wounds."

"Amen," Ben said.

Epilogue

"Ladies, are we ready?" Bitsy Harmony asked. Flora Downey, Anna Carter and the rest of the Paradise Ladies' Auxiliary nodded as they adjusted the sashes on their pale pink attendant dresses. They followed Bitsy through the open French doors of the clinic chapel, down the stone pavers and past the rows of guests, to stand with bouquets of wildflowers in hand around the gazebo.

Once they were in position, Bitsy nodded and the chapel organ began. The lilting, sweet melody of the processional filled the courtyard.

Sara turned to the man in the wheelchair beside her.

"Ready, Uncle Henry?"

"Indeed I am, dear. I've waited for this since the moment I met your groom."

"How did you know, Uncle Henry? I don't think I really knew until I saw the garden."

"I recognized something of myself in Ben, I think."

"Ready?" he asked his niece.

"More than ready," she said with a smile.

They began the short walk down the path, which had been widened to allow Henry to roam around the chapel garden with ease.

Sara glanced at the guests as they turned to smile at her as she walked slowly past. Rows of satin-covered chairs were filled with citizens of Paradise, dear friends, family and colleagues.

When they reached the halfway point, Henry stopped and lifted her hand, turning his niece over to her father. Sara reached down to kiss her uncle.

How blessed she was to be given away to the man she loved by the two men who had raised her.

Sara smiled tenderly at her father. Today he wore a white Stetson that emphasized the healthy tan he had since starting back to work. He was here today thanks to Ben, who had overcome his own fears to save Hollis Elliott's life.

They reached the steps of the gazebo, and her father walked up the two short steps to the landing. Large tulle and satin bows of ivory and coral decorated the hand railings.

Her father kissed her cheek and gently placed her hand in Ben's before he stepped back and sat down.

Only now did she dare to glance up at her groom. She knew her heart was bursting, and she wanted to see him, to sear the memory of his face at this very moment before they sealed their love on her heart forever.

Sara looked up. The lean, dark, serious doctor she fell in love with was smiling, with a tiny sparkle of amusement in his eyes. He was happy. She liked it when Ben was happy. There was no doubt in her mind that he loved her, completely and totally.

He didn't even realize it, but not only had Ben Rogers slain dragons for her, he had helped her grow into the woman and doctor whom her mother and father could be proud of.

Thank You, dear Lord, for this wonderful partner and colleague. Amen.

* * * * *

If you enjoyed this story by Tina Radcliffe, be sure to check out the other Love Inspired books this month!

Dear Reader,

Welcome to Paradise. I hope you enjoyed Ben and Sara's story. They're head-smart physicians who must learn to listen to their spirit and the leading of the Lord, who will never let them down. As we all do, they find themselves struggling with fear and condemnation and getting a little lost on the path to God's perfect plan for their lives. During those times we are the most confused, the answer is simple: trust in the Lord for the answer.

I never actually planned to write a medical story, but now that I look back, I think all my stories, published and unpublished, have a medical thread. I just didn't realize it. When the editors at Love Inspired asked me to consider writing a book with a medical theme, I knew I was ready.

Drop me a line and let me know what you think. I can be reached at tina@tinaradcliffe. com or through my website, www.tinaradcliffe.com.

Tina Radcliffe

Questions for Discussion

1. The theme of *Mending the Doctor's Heart* is trusting in the Lord. If you are accustomed to relying solely upon your intellect, a step of faith can be difficult. Can you relate to this?

2. Both Ben Rogers and Sara Elliott are starting over. Have you ever experienced a starting-over point in your life?

3. Ben feels responsible for his sister's death. While not logical, this guilt has given him a phobia. Have you ever known anyone with a phobia?

4. Despite Ben's phobia about hospitals and treating patients, opportunities continue to present themselves where he must treat the injured. Could this be God's intervention to show Ben His will for his medical career? What do you think?

5. Bitsy Harmony is a colorful secondary character who leads the Paradise Ladies' Auxiliary. What did you think of her?

6. Sara's father, Hollis, is a very controlling man. Can you understand how his fears have shaped his personality?

7. Paradise, Colorado, is a fictional small mountain town located near the real cities of Monte Vista and South Fork. Have you ever been to Colorado? You can find out more about this area at http://www.southfork.org/index.asp.

8. Rural medicine can be challenging because there are less resources for medical professionals, along with environmental obstacles. Are you familiar with the term rural medicine?

9. Ben and Sara have both experienced loss, but they respond differently, possibly due to time. Do you think the phrase "time heals all wounds" has merit?

10. Another theme in *Mending the Doctor's Heart* is forgiveness. Ben struggles to forgive himself, and Sara deals with forgiving her father. Forgiveness is an act of faith. Do you agree with this?

11. Ben's plan in Paradise is isolation, but the Lord has other plans. Have you ever found yourself chased down by the Lord's plan for your life?

12. Uncle Henry is a spiritual mentor for both Ben and Sara. Have you ever had a spiritual mentor in your life?

13. Sara believes that people are more important than things. Have you ever known anyone who has their priorities backward and puts things before the people in their life?

14. The chapel garden is a gift from Ben to Sara. He gives up his material possessions to make it a reality. What do you think of this gift of the heart?

LARGER-PRINT BOOKS!

GET 2 FREE LARGER-PRINT NOVELS PLUS 2 FREE MYSTERY GIFTS

Love Inspired

Larger-print novels are now available...

YES! Please send me 2 FREE LARGER-PRINT Love Inspired® novels and my 2 FREE mystery gifts (gifts are worth about $10). After receiving them, if I don't wish to receive any more books, I can return the shipping statement marked "cancel." If I don't cancel, I will receive 6 brand-new novels every month and be billed just $4.99 per book in the U.S. or $5.49 per book in Canada. That's a savings of at least 23% off the cover price. It's quite a bargain! Shipping and handling is just 50¢ per book in the U.S. and 75¢ per book in Canada.* I understand that accepting the 2 free books and gifts places me under no obligation to buy anything. I can always return a shipment and cancel at any time. Even if I never buy another book, the two free books and gifts are mine to keep forever.

122/322 IDN FVY7

Name _____ (PLEASE PRINT) _____

Address _____ Apt. # _____

City _____ State/Prov. _____ Zip/Postal Code _____

Signature (if under 18, a parent or guardian must sign)

Mail to the Harlequin® Reader Service:
IN U.S.A.: P.O. Box 1867, Buffalo, NY 14240-1867
IN CANADA: P.O. Box 609, Fort Erie, Ontario L2A 5X3

Are you a current subscriber to Love Inspired books and want to receive the larger-print edition?
Call 1-800-873-8635 or visit www.ReaderService.com.

* Terms and prices subject to change without notice. Prices do not include applicable taxes. Sales tax applicable in N.Y. Canadian residents will be charged applicable taxes. Offer not valid in Quebec. This offer is limited to one order per household. Not valid for current subscribers to Love Inspired Larger Print books. All orders subject to credit approval. Credit or debit balances in a customer's account(s) may be offset by any other outstanding balance owed by or to the customer. Please allow 4 to 6 weeks for delivery. Offer available while quantities last.

Your Privacy—The Harlequin® Reader Service is committed to protecting your privacy. Our Privacy Policy is available online at www.ReaderService.com or upon request from the Harlequin Reader Service.

We make a portion of our mailing list available to reputable third parties that offer products we believe may interest you. If you prefer that we not exchange your name with third parties, or if you wish to clarify or modify your communication preferences, please visit us at www.ReaderService.com/consumerschoice or write to us at Harlequin Reader Service Preference Service, P.O. Box 9062, Buffalo, NY 14269. Include your complete name and address.

LILPDIR13

LARGER-PRINT BOOKS!

GET 2 FREE
LARGER-PRINT NOVELS
PLUS 2 FREE
MYSTERY GIFTS

Love Inspired®

SUSPENSE
RIVETING INSPIRATIONAL ROMANCE

Larger-print novels are now available...

Reader Service.com

Manage your account online!

- Review your order history
- Manage your payments
- Update your address

*We've designed
the Harlequin® Reader Service
website just for you.*

Enjoy all the features!

- Reader excerpts from any series
- Respond to mailings and special monthly offers
- Discover new series available to you
- Browse the Bonus Bucks catalog
- Share your feedback

Visit us at:
ReaderService.com